About Last Night

Caitlin Ricci

Published by
DREAMSPINNER PRESS

5032 Capital Circle SW, Suite 2, PMB# 279, Tallahassee, FL 32305-7886 USA
www.dreamspinnerpress.com

ISBN: 978-1-63476-873-3
Digital ISBN: 978-1-63476-874-0
Library of Congress Control Number: 2016900170
Published April 2016
v. 1.0

Printed in the United States of America
∞
This paper meets the requirements of
ANSI/NISO Z39.48-1992 (Permanence of Paper).

Readers love *One More Time* by CAITLIN RICCI

"I had a blast with this story… It caught my attention from the moment I started reading and kept it all the way to the end."
—MM Good Book Reviews

"The writing is great, the characters interesting…"
—Three Books Over the Rainbow

"I loved the feel-good hometown. I love the setting in the Rockies and I love watching Caleb make the transition from LA life to small-town living."
—Inked Rainbow Reviews

"*One More Time* is definitely worth the chance... It is definitely not a pretty or fluffy scenario and it is not hearts and flowers. It is men, being men, and trying to traverse through their feelings."
—QUEERcentric

"It was excellently written, and Caitlin made sure not to rush..."
—Just Love

One
More
Time

A Thornwood Novel

Caitlin Ricci

By CAITLIN RICCI

Blood Slave
Country Strong
Cuddling (Dreamspinner Anthology)
For the Asking
His Lion Tamer
Marked by Grief
With Cari Z: Worth the Wait

A FOREVER HOME
Rescuing Jack
Of Monsters and Men

A PLANET CALLED WISH
To the Highest Bidder
Fantasy for a Gentleman

THORNWOOD
One More Time
About Last Night

Published by Harmony Ink Press
Crush
First Time for Everything (Harmony Ink Anthology)
Weathering the Storm

Published by DREAMSPINNER PRESS
www.dreamspinnerpress.com

Scott, I love you. Thank you for keeping me on track,
for the motivation, and for always giving me new story ideas.

AUTHOR'S NOTE

Welcome back to Thornwood.

CHAPTER ONE

LOSING MY virginity to a stranger the night before my first semester in college was probably the stupidest idea my friends and I had ever come up with. And I wished they were here with me now as I fixed a simple black mask over my face and headed up the steps to what was supposed to be the best party on campus for the whole year. My friends, stuck in Colorado while I was here in Miami, would have egged me on. They would have been encouraging. I could have stood by them and laughed like I actually had some friends instead of coming into the fraternity and standing awkwardly in the corner with a drink someone had pushed into my hand.

I was from a small town in the Colorado mountains so I'd had a drink before, but I wasn't big on them. If I really was going to go through with this, though, I knew I'd need some courage, so I started drinking whatever it was in big gulps. It hurt, and it burned, but I was able to keep it down, and when I was done with my first, I grabbed another. Smiling at the people around me was easier after that first drink. Laughing came next, and talking about classes, the Miami humidity, and how I'd only just seen the ocean for the first time was almost fun.

I'd never been all that great at dancing, but with the alcohol working its way through me, that didn't seem to matter so much anymore. Rock mixed with punk, which bled quickly into pop as the house thumped around me. People laughed, and I danced with anyone who wanted to be close to me. Maybe if I'd been sober or had less outgoing friends, maybe then the idea of getting rid of my virginity before anyone found out I hadn't had sex yet wouldn't have made as much sense. But the guys had told me how all their college friends only wanted them because they were cute and inexperienced and how I didn't want to lose my virginity to someone like that.

As the night wore on, it started to make more and more sense to me. I was eighteen, fairly cute according to my friends, and if I wasn't worried about who to give my virginity to, and making it count as something important, then I could have fun and not be worried about dating or who I was having sex with now that I wasn't living at home.

I saw the perfect guy sitting on the kitchen island. His legs dangled over the side, and he had a drink in his hand too. My third, maybe, was nearly out, and I'd come in to see about getting another. This guy had nice thick thighs, a bit of hair showing under his shorts, and a Miami College T-shirt on. It was purple, just like the mask he had on that hid most of his face from me. It did nothing to cover up the bright bleach-blond hair sticking up all over his head or his pretty green eyes.

I danced up to him, thinking I looked cool as hell, and he just laughed at me. We were alone in the kitchen, for the moment, when I moved between his legs and leaned up to kiss him. My glass fell over the side of the counter, and he must've set his down somewhere because he put his arms around me, and then his tongue went into my mouth. I sucked on his lower lip and rubbed my stomach against the front of his shorts. He never pushed me away, never even seemed like he might not have been interested, and I thought he was practically perfect.

We traded kisses with my hands on the tops of his thighs until people came into the kitchen. We broke apart then, and I was feeling a little dizzy, but when he took my hand and pulled me through the house, past couples making out over every inch of available space and into a large closet, I didn't worry about a thing.

We kept kissing, and he ran his hands over me roughly, as if he couldn't get enough of me. That's the same way I felt about him in that moment, like I needed everything and then some, like there wasn't enough air in the closet, and I was burning up. He reached for my pants, but I had my hands on his first and dropped to my knees in front of him. Without a word I took him into my mouth, sliding my lips over his thick head, as he rested his hands on the back of my neck. This part was familiar to me. I'd been giving head for years. He didn't push me down, didn't try to control me in any way, just rested there as I licked up the underside of his cock and jacked him with one hand while touching myself with the other.

After a few minutes, and getting to taste his salty precum, I got up, and he turned me around, pushing me onto something hard, and I realized it wasn't a closet we were in, but actually the laundry room. Huh. I'd never considered my first time to be while I was bent over a dryer. But it didn't really bother me, either. I was grinning as he pushed down my pants and spread me open for him.

At least one of us was sober enough to remember to use a condom, I thought as I heard him tear one open. A little stretching, not nearly as much as I needed, but at least the alcohol dulled the pain, and then I felt him inside of me. I gasped, he groaned, and I leaned forward as he put one hand on my shoulder, right next to my neck, and the other on my hip.

I was lucky to find someone that was gay, bi, or too drunk to care right off the bat. And God he was hot too, all hard muscle and strong fingers that gripped my shoulder.

"Oh fuck," he groaned, the first words he'd said to me.

I laughed, though it came out as more of a pant, and nodded as he fucked me against the dryer. I'd be sore in the morning, I was sure, but right then, in that moment, I thought everything was wonderful. My friends were right. This was the best way to lose my virginity. And, even with my limited experience in the department, I thought purple-mask guy was fucking amazing.

"Right there," I gasped out when he hit something inside of me that felt pretty perfect.

He hit it again, and I shook. He laughed, and I leaned all the way onto the dryer and gripped it as tight as I could, my fingers curling around the edges. It didn't matter that I didn't know his name or what he looked like or anything else about him. It was almost better, actually. There were no expectations here, no complications either. It was just pleasure and excitement.

The cold metal bled into me, mixing with the heat of my skin, and I instantly loved the feeling it created over me. He moved his hand from my shoulder to the back of my hair as he got closer. I was pretty sure, from the times I'd jacked off with my friends, that his jerky, erratic movements meant that he was getting close, and I grabbed my cock to keep up with him. I wanted to come too, and with him in me still. I sped up, nearly to the point where I'd be causing myself pain, before I released with a shudder onto the front of the dryer.

I was still a bit limp as I recovered when he pushed himself all the way inside of me and yanked back on my hair. He pumped into me, and I could feel his cock pulsing inside as he held me there. After a few seconds, he let my hair go, and I slumped forward.

I thought he'd leave me for sure after that. We were done, but he apparently wasn't, as he turned me back over and helped me sit up on the dryer. It was cold on my ass, but he warmed me right up again with his rough kisses.

"Thanks," I said to him, when he let me up to breathe.

"Yeah. You too."

He gave me another kiss and licked at my bottom lip before leaving me in that laundry room. I didn't go after him, didn't try to find him again at the party, just cleaned up my mess with a rag I tossed into the washer as soon as I was done, fixed my pants, then walked back to my hotel.

I was moving into the dorms in the morning and felt pretty good about the night I'd had. It was nearly eleven, but in Colorado it was only getting to nine, so once I was back in my hotel room and showered, I called my mom.

"Hey, sweetie pie. How's Miami?" she asked me as soon as she picked up.

I tossed the towel I'd been using on my hair to the side and stretched out on the bed. "Pretty decent. Lots of humidity. And a lot of people in this hotel seem to have little dogs. Maybe it's a Miami thing because I'm pretty sure no one in town has a dog under five pounds back home."

My mom laughed, and it was good to hear her voice. "No. I think we'd call them bear food if someone did. Oh, your cousin Trent says hello."

He wasn't really my cousin. My mom just worked at the same diner for the past twenty years that Trent's mom had owned. We were cousins because our moms had been best friends before his mom had passed. "Say hi back for me, please." I liked Trent. He was a cop, but he didn't pull us over unless we were being stupid. I hadn't had a car when I'd left town for Miami so my record was thankfully clean. But a lot of my friends had had to take summer jobs to pay off their tickets for being reckless.

I hoped she couldn't tell I'd been drinking. I'd only been drunk a few times before, but I was pretty sure this was one of them. I didn't feel sick, yet, but I knew I needed to take some painkillers tonight to hold off what was certainly coming for me in the morning. Whatever, it would be completely worth it for the night I'd had.

"Are you staying out of trouble?"

I laughed. "Yeah. More or less."

She laughed with me, and I was glad we had the kind of relationship that, if I'd wanted to, I could have told her about my night and she would have only worried about me using protection. She was really cool like that. "Your dad made you a mixed tape, CD, MP3 thing... anyway. It's all the songs about Miami that he could find. He's going to send it to you in the mail. Some of them, though.... Thomas, honey, there are days I'm glad you are only interested in boys."

I shook my head as I laughed. "Men mom. I'm eighteen. I like men now. Not boys." I stared up at the ceiling.

"Oh, excuse me. Look who's all grown up now just because they got to move out. Well, I'm glad you like men, then, because some of these songs about women and their thongs and booties.... I may not be on top of all of what you kids do or know, but even I know that when that song said booty it wasn't talking about those cute little socks I knitted for Elijah."

"Yeah. Probably not. How's the baby anyway?" He was almost a year old now, my little foster brother. I called him a baby because he was so tiny, but really he was getting up there and growing a bit more every day. Maybe he was still a baby.

I heard the sadness in my mom's voice and could picture her frown as if I was sitting right there next to her. "Oh, you know. He's a handful. Those damn drugs…."

I nodded. I'd taken my first sip of alcohol with my friends in one of their dad's man caves while we were in middle school, but I'd been really careful never to get involved with any kinds of drugs because I saw what they did to the babies my mom fostered. It wasn't that I planned to ever have kids, biologically anyway, but I just didn't want to be a part of something that hurt babies so much.

"I'm sure it's tough. Are you still thinking about taking in those brothers too?" I asked her. My mom was always fostering more kids. There were a few she'd adopted over the years, like me, but most of them were only with her during their court cases or before they got placed with a family member.

"With you out of the house, it seems like someone should be using your room. I can't very well make Saturday morning pancake shapes for just your dad and me."

God I missed Saturday morning pancakes already. My mom put cinnamon in the pancakes then dusted them with sugar. She used real butter too, the kind she made from shaking heavy whipping cream in a mason jar until it got all hard. My stomach growled, even though I'd had a cheeseburger, and I rubbed it. I'd only been gone a few days, but I was already missing home.

"I can't wait to come have them again. Missing you and Dad already." I frowned, wondering if I'd really been ready to move across the country. I'd considered all of the colleges in Denver, but I'd wanted to be by the ocean and see something more than the mountains for once.

"Oh honey, we miss you too. Don't you worry, I'll still be making pancakes when you come back for fall break. Or winter break or whenever really. Don't feel like you need to rush back home. Go, have an adventure. Fall in love, break some hearts, taste the ocean for me."

I wiped at my eyes because they were blurry and realized I was crying without even meaning to or knowing that I was doing it. "Love you, Mama."

"Love you too, Thomas. Now, it's after eleven there, if this world clock we set to Miami time is correct, so I'm going to let you go get some rest so that you can move in bright and early tomorrow. Take pictures for me, and make sure to lift with your legs, not your back. You don't need to be rushed to the emergency room before school even starts. Blow up something in the chemistry lab first."

I grinned and sighed. "You'd be so worried."

"But I would also have the first son in Thornwood to blow up a chemistry lab. Think of that now. All the ladies at the diner asked about you today. They think you'll come back all tanned and ready for their daughters. Come back with some handsome man instead. That'll show them."

"I'll try," I promised her. Still smiling, I thought about the guy from the party. Of course I'd never see him again, but it had been fun. If she told her diner friends about what I'd done, that would certainly give them something to talk about, or more like gossip about, in the tiny town I'd lived in all my life before coming here. "Talk to you later." I yawned, really feeling the time now.

"Night, baby. You take care of yourself, and remember to send me pictures."

"I will. I will. Promise." We blew each other kisses through the phone, and I hung up. An old movie on the TV to help me go to sleep and I was out less than an hour later.

Chapter Two

I'D BEEN on some small college campuses before, back when I was maybe considering a school in Denver, but I liked Miami College's campus a lot more than any I'd seen in Denver. There were lots of palm trees, which we didn't have in Colorado, and lush grass that wasn't covered with pine needles and the tracks of foxes and raccoons that were trying to get into our garbage cans overnight. I had two suitcases and a really heavy duffel bag, which I thought had been a lot of stuff, but as I saw people unloading rental vans, my perspective on that changed pretty quickly.

There was sort of a mini orientation to go to first, in which I sat down with a bunch of people who looked around my age but were all too nervous to make conversation first. I sat. I listened to the basic rules of the dorm and knew I wouldn't be having an issue, at least on my side, since I wouldn't be bringing alcohol or drugs into the dorms. I didn't know about my roommate, of course, but I really hoped he wasn't the kind of guy to be partying all night and expecting me to join in.

After we'd all been sufficiently warned about what would get us thrown out, we were put into lines. I handed over my immunization records, shook hands with someone who I guessed was in charge of the dorms, then was given a key and a map and sent on my way with a quick "Good luck this year."

My dorm wasn't all that hard to find, and I got to walk by a large fountain to get to it. I hoped my classes took me past it most days because I wouldn't have minded the view at all. There were even some ducks in it, swimming around and diving. It was pretty cute. I went to the wrong floor first before I figured out the number system in the dorm, then found my room easily enough too.

It was nice, as far as a first place went, with two beds, a desk, and a sink in front of the bathroom that had a full shower in it. I was happy with that since that meant I could brush my teeth in the morning and not have to worry about coordinating my dental hygiene with someone else's shower. There was a counter but no real kitchen. We had a microwave, though, and I knew from the map I'd been mailed there were plenty of places to eat on campus. We had a minifridge too. I considered waiting for my roommate to see which bed he'd want, but I didn't want to be sitting around for hours doing nothing, either. So I chose the one to the left and started unpacking my things.

I was glad I hadn't waited to put my stuff away because my roommate didn't come in for another two hours, and he was pulling a dolly full of totes behind him that the small dorm room might not have had space for if my things weren't completely out of the way. I didn't want to start tripping over each other already since I was sure that there would be a lot of that happening at some point during the year. I got off my bed, where I'd been reading since my things had been organized over an hour before, and stuck out my hand to introduce myself. Only I stopped short with my hand hanging between us as I thought I recognized him.

"Hey, I'm Rem Daniels. It's short for Remington. I guess you're my new roommate for the year," he said, and shook my hand while I was staring at him and pulled in his stuff. He locked the door behind himself and started spreading out his totes. "Can you believe this heat? Crazy, right?" He shook his head, and I watched him go sit on his bed. It still needed sheets and a pillow, but he didn't seem to mind as he lay back and brought one of his legs up.

"What's your name?" he turned his head and asked me.

His question broke me out of my stupor and I started noticing the little things about him that I'd liked so much the night before. His smile was a dead giveaway, though. "Thomas Maloney. I think we've met before actually." I waited to see if he would recognize me, if he'd been paying as much attention to me last night as I had been to him. I wasn't naive enough to think that last night was some magical thing that actually meant something between us. I got rid of my virginity with a stranger, and he got a hookup in the laundry room of a fraternity with a guy wearing a mask. I'd never expected shaking mountains or rainbows and unicorns or something like that. But I kind of wanted him to at least acknowledge the fact that we'd had sex. That shouldn't have been too much to ask for.

"Really? We have? Did you grow up in Tallahassee?"

I crossed my arms over my chest and shook my head. "Colorado, actually. Little town called Thornwood."

He gave me a smile, and it was the same one he had the night before when he'd been kissing me, after he'd just come while still inside me. I knew it was him for sure now. "Ah. A country boy."

"We met last night at the party." I thought that might jog his memory, but he only shrugged.

"Maybe. There were a lot of people there. And I was pretty wasted. I don't remember much at all."

I sat down on my bed with my feet pulled under me, and leaned toward him. "So you don't remember the laundry room?"

"Nope." He shook his head, but I did see a little blush come over his cheeks.

When he blushed I knew I had him. "And you don't remember me on my knees, my mouth around your cock either probably? Or you bending me over the dryer, your hand in my hair, your other hand on my hip? I've got some faint bruises if you want to see them."

He had his mouth open, just slightly, as he stared at me. "Oh shit."

"Last night it was 'oh fuck,'" I said with a smile.

"You can't tell anyone." He sat up and stared right back at me. "Not anyone. Not at all."

I shrugged. "That's fine. I wasn't going to go shooting off my mouth anyway. Why'd you pretend not to recognize me? It wasn't that hard to tell who you were."

"It wasn't? I thought dying my hair and wearing a mask would have helped."

10

He had changed his hair color. It was a curly dark brown with red highlights now. And it matched his eyebrows, which I hadn't been able to see before. He must have had to use a ton of gel crap in it to make it stand up in spikes as much as it had been the night before. "I recognized your smile."

He nodded and rocked a little on his bed. "So...."

"Yeah."

"You sure that you won't tell anyone?"

I shook my head. "Of course not. We had sex. That's not that big of a deal. I was just mad that you pretended not to recognize me."

Laughing, he got off the bed and started opening his totes. "Yeah. I recognized you. Kind of hard not to. Just...." He looked away from his totes to meet my gaze again. "Thanks for not telling anyone."

"Sure. Thanks for being a good first time for me." I figured he was probably in the closet and didn't want to be outed his first semester of college. I got that. I'd never been in the closet, but then again not everyone had the kind of mom like I did—she started getting the numbers of the cute guys we saw for me starting when I was twelve.

He stared at me for a while, until I started to get uncomfortable with all of his attention being focused on me. "That was your first time? Seriously?"

I nodded. "Yeah. So thanks." I shrugged. With my mom getting me guys' numbers and my dad buying me condoms well before I started high school, sex had never been all that big of a deal for me. I'd had plenty of opportunities, and my parents' wishes to be safe and have fun, so I could have had sex at any time. But in high school, there'd been no one all that special. And I didn't want to wait for that special person in college too. I didn't want to be a twenty-two-year-old virgin when I walked away with my bachelor's degree in a few years.

He shook his head and started pulling out his books. "Why in the hell would you lose your virginity to a stranger at a party? I could have been anybody. I could have been some sick, twisted perv."

If he thought I was a complete idiot, he didn't know me at all. Well, actually, he didn't. "If you had been, I've got mace. Always have it on me. And so what? I wanted to get rid of it and be just like everyone else here. No virginity, no hang-ups when it came to sex, no worries. My friends suggested it, and I'm glad they did."

"Your friends are idiots."

Well, that wasn't entirely wrong, but I still felt the need to defend them anyway. "You don't even know them."

He shook his head and went back to unpacking. "Don't need to."

God he was cute, though. He'd been hot last night as he'd thrust against me and dug his short fingernails into my hip, but now, as I saw him go through his books and an entire tub of power muscle drinks, I thought he was pretty adorable. "I like your hair more this way."

"Huh?" he asked me.

Maybe he hadn't heard me. "Your hair." I touched my own. It was short, dark blond, and didn't ever do anything it was supposed to. His curled around his forehead.

With a nod he went back to unpacking. "Thanks. I change it sometimes with highlights and things. The red isn't real. My natural color is closer to yours but more brown."

"Yeah." I took off my shirt and lay back on my bed to keep reading. "So, you're okay living with someone for a year who you had sex with?" I asked him.

"Yep. You?"

I nodded without looking over at him. "Yeah."

"It'll take any awkwardness about us being naked around each other away pretty quickly."

I liked the way he thought. "Absolutely." We shared a quick grin, and then I went back to reading, and he kept unloading his totes.

I was thirty pages further into the novel when my phone started ringing. "Hey, Mom," I said, answering it right away.

"How's my baby? How's your dorm?"

I looked around the room and shrugged. "It's pretty decent. Nice first place away from home." I rolled over onto my stomach, put the book aside, and blushed when the bed squeaked under me, making me think of sex.

I glanced over at Rem to find him watching me as well. I was pretty sure he was thinking the same thing as me, and that made me smile.

"Well, good. We're so proud of you for going to college out of state, even if you only do it for a semester. It's good for you to see the world. Have you gone swimming in the ocean yet?"

Laughing, I shook my head. "I haven't really had time. I promise, though, I will go swimming here soon."

"In the ocean."

"Yes, yes. I'll go swimming in the ocean. I'll tell you how it tastes and feels, and I'll try not to get eaten by a great white shark while I'm at it."

She laughed. "Yes, don't get eaten by a shark. What's your roommate like?"

I turned to look back at Rem, who was drinking a muscle drink for some reason. It said it was banana flavored, though I could smell it from across the room, and it smelled like baby vomit. The little bit that was on his lip when he pulled it away from his mouth looked like vomit too. Completely gross.

"Oh, he's cute enough. Curly hair. More muscles than I've got. Maybe he's a bodybuilder."

Rem stuck his tongue out at me, and I pulled my feet up so that I could cross them at my ankles and hang them over my butt. "Football, actually," he said.

"Oh, Mom. He says he plays football. I'm rooming with a jock."

She laughed. "Didn't you used to have a crush on that one running quarter person, the one with the long hair?"

It took me a minute to figure out what she was getting at. "Wide receiver. The one that plays for the Demons. Yeah, I remember. He still plays for them actually. At least I still think he still does." With Rem watching me closely and smiling around his muscle drink, I was kind of regretting telling my mom about my crush last year.

"Ask your roommate who he wants to play for or if he wants to play professionally at all," she told me.

I turned on my side to be able to see him better. "My mom wants to know if you're going to try to play professionally, and if so, who do you want to play for?"

"I do, and whoever will sign me," he said right away.

"Oh he even sounds cute. You're going to be in so much trouble if he's as cute as he sounds."

Of course my mom would say that. "Nope, it's worse," I told her while still looking at Rem. He finished off his drink and got up to throw it away in the little trash bin that had come with the room.

I heard her laughing through the phone and was pretty sure most of Thornwood could hear that cackle too. "Oh, my poor baby. You'd better be careful, then. Send me some pictures of him too, okay?"

"Yeah, yeah. I'll take lots of pictures for you."

"Good. I've got to head into work for the dinner shift. I'll talk to you later, okay, baby?"

I nodded, even though she couldn't see me do it. "Yep. Have fun at the diner."

"I always do. You know it's just like hanging out with friends for me."

Yeah, I did know that. It's why she was so good at her job and made some pretty great tips. She wouldn't quit that job for the world because she loved it so much. "Bye, Mom."

"Bye, baby. Be good."

"Will do." I hung up and saw Rem watching me from across the room. "Hi."

He came over, and I thought he was going to go to his totes that still needed to be unpacked, but instead he bent over me and gave me a quick kiss. It wasn't anything like the needy kisses we'd shared last night, but it reminded me of them well enough. I reached for him, but he was pulling away from me before I could get my hands on him to keep him close. "So I'm cuter than I sound, then?"

I groaned and blushed deeply. "You heard all of that?"

"Yeah. And you have a thing for Reggie Delica? Not saying he's not good-looking, but you could have chosen someone with a better record."

Rolling my eyes, I smiled at him. "I'm not really watching him for his record when he runs around in those white pants." I licked my lips just thinking about him bent over on the field.

"Yeah, I know. They're pretty sexy."

I went back to reading since I wanted to finish this novel before I had to start reading books for class. *The Mysteries of Bell Creek* was my favorite series about this gay detective and how he went through different worlds, all linked back to Bell Creek. It was sometimes dark, usually pretty sexy, and I liked that Detective Cast always won. There was something like sixteen books in the series, and I was only on the seventh with more coming out each year. I needed to read fast if I had any hope of catching up.

But Rem distracted me by coming over and running his fingers down my spine. He put his hand over the waist of my jeans and gave them a little tug. "I'm all done unpacking. Want to redo last night without the masks?"

Of course I did. Rem was hot, and I wanted him. But I was still a bit sore. "Can't right now. Can I blow you instead?"

He didn't look disappointed at my offer, but he did look curious about why I couldn't have sex with him right then as I put my bookmark back into my book—I never dog-eared my pages—and slid from my bed to the floor in front of him.

"Why not?" he asked me as I undid his belt buckle and put my hand inside his pants to get to his cock. He rocked forward, leaning over me.

I gave him a little smile and put my free hand inside my pants. "Because I'm a bit sore still from having you fuck me so hard. Don't get me wrong, I loved last night, but I need a little time to recover."

He moved his hand to my cheek as I leaned toward him and took him between my lips. It was nice to be able to experience this and feel him against my tongue without the alcohol in my system to make everything fuzzy in my mind.

"Sorry. I should have known somehow. But I was pretty wasted, and you didn't act like a virgin. You still don't." I took him to his base, and he groaned and moved his hand to the back of my head. "Fuck." He pushed a little forward, and I moved my hand that wasn't around my own cock to cup his balls and squeeze them as gently as I could. He tightened his hand in my hair, and I pulled my lips over him as I came back up to take a deep breath.

"There's no way you're a virgin when you can deep throat like that."

I rolled my eyes at him and stroked my hand over his cock. "You're not the first guy I've sucked, just the first I let into my ass."

"Ah."

"Yeah." I was a little annoyed that he'd thought I'd lied to him, but maybe he hadn't meant it like that. Maybe he'd just been so stunned at my skills with my mouth that he'd said it, even if it sounded stupid.

Instead of dwelling on it, I went back to enjoying what I was doing. He wasn't the biggest guy I'd ever sucked or the longest, but he did make the best noises, and thankfully he kept his hair pretty trimmed up. It wasn't long before he was thrusting into my mouth and spilling into my throat. I hadn't meant to swallow him, but I didn't really mind it since he tasted okay. With pot legal in Colorado, there were plenty of guys I'd sucked that tasted disgusting right after smoking it. I didn't even gag on him, which I was pretty proud about.

When he tried to move back, I grabbed his butt with my free hand and held him there. I wanted to come with him in my mouth, just like I had with him in my butt last night. It didn't take me long either, and thankfully our floor was some cheap linoleum that was easy to clean up because I sprayed over it as I jerked myself off.

I let him go, and he moved back a little, giving me some room. I was up and moving around a few seconds later, and I had the floor cleaned up in no time. "Thanks for that," I told him once I was done.

"Thank you. How long have you been giving head anyway?"

I shrugged and lay back down on my bed. He was still standing in the middle of the room where I'd left him, but he had fixed his pants at least. "Few years. I started when I was fourteen."

"And you're how old now?"

I had my book open to where I'd left off. "Eighteen. You?"

"Nineteen. Damn you're good."

His compliment made me blush. I didn't get complimented like that back home, and it was nice to hear. "Thanks, so are you." He gave me a quick smile, then went over to his bed and pulled a laptop out of his backpack. I relaxed on the bed with my feet hanging over my butt and kept reading.

CHAPTER THREE

I WAS more than halfway done with my novel and perfectly content to stay on my bed and relax for the rest of the afternoon when I saw Rem put his laptop aside and pull out another of those gross drinks.

"Lunch," he told me, when I met his gaze.

I shuddered. "Do all your meals come out of bottles?"

He gave me a grin and finished off the bottle before answering me. "Nope. Well, not usually. I'm not the starting quarterback for the Crusaders yet, and I want to gain some more muscle and get better so that the coach will consider putting me in as the starter, even though it's my freshman year. Pro team coaches notice that kind of thing."

If he said so. Personally I thought he looked just fine, but then again I wasn't a football coach. I was only some guy who liked having sex with him and liked what I saw in the little patches of his naked skin he'd shown me. I hadn't gotten to have him completely naked, not yet anyway, but since we'd known each other less than twenty-four hours, I figured there would be plenty of time for that soon.

I still hadn't put my shirt back on yet. I didn't really see a reason to, and when I turned over onto my back I caught him watching me. Sure, I'd just come and so had he, but that didn't mean I was completely satisfied. Not in a big way. I unbuttoned my pants and moved them a little down my hips.

"There, that's better," I said as casually as I could. "They're a little tight sometimes." They really weren't. If anything they were too big on me as they hung off my hips and showed off the fact that I really didn't like wearing underwear of any kind.

"Uh-huh." He licked his lips, and I was pretty sure he didn't believe me. But since he didn't come over and take my pants the rest of the way off, maybe I was wrong.

THAI FOOD arrived, courtesy of my mom and dad and the restaurant down the street, just after two. "You seem pretty close to your mom," Rem said later that afternoon when I'd gotten off the phone with her again, thanking her for feeding us both. She didn't have to, and I told her that, but I figured every once in a while we'd have food waiting for us. She'd ordered my favorites, and I hungrily dug into the summer rolls with a deliciously spicy peanut sauce.

"Yeah, I'm close to both of them. Sorry if Thai isn't something you like." We were sitting on the floor with the food spread out between us and our backs on our beds. I'd said it, even though I was watching him slurp down some pad Thai, as if he hadn't eaten in days.

He shook his head and took another big bite. "No. I love it. Though I've never had the parents of a guy I fucked buy me lunch."

I didn't mind his language or the heat in his eyes when he looked at me. I gave him a smile. "First for me too."

He returned my smile, and we ate quickly because we were both so hungry. We were done and cleaning up when someone knocked on the door. "More food?" I wondered aloud, thinking maybe my mom had thought to order us dessert too. Not that I didn't like Chinese fortune cookies, but when my fortune was "The sun will shine tomorrow" that wasn't all that helpful to me. Something closer to how to pass all of my classes this semester would be a much more appreciated hint.

Rem was closer to the door, so he went to it, and I was treated to the oh-so-lovely surprise of a girl with gorgeous blonde hair running into his arms. She gave him a big hug, and he actually lifted her up to give her one of those romance movie twirls.

Please be his sister. Oh God, please for the love of fuck be his sister. Nope. Not his sister, I decided pretty quickly as I saw them kiss.

I was still staring at them when they pulled apart, and she giggled as she leaned against his side and hugged his upper arm.

"Thomas, this is my girlfriend, Angela. Babe, this is my new roommate." I saw desperation there behind his easy smile and too-bright eyes. He was keeping this secret and begging me to as well without saying a word.

Okay, I could do this, I decided. Sure. I forced a smile I hoped didn't look too fake and came forward to shake her hand. Her fingers were warm and delicate against my palm. I was fine shaking her hand, but she took it a step further and came at me for a hug. Her smile was so bright it was hard not to like her instantly, and I hugged her back when her arms came around me and looked over her head at Rem. He still looked so scared. I shook my head, hoping he understood. We'd had anonymous sex, and I'd sucked him off. It didn't mean we were dating or anything even close to it. It did mean he was an ass for cheating on his girlfriend with me, though. They might have an open relationship, but the way he was looking at me, I was fairly certain that wasn't what was going on here.

Angela stepped out of my arms and went right back to Rem. "Okay, so show me around your dorm. And let's go get something to eat. I'm starving. Tell me you haven't eaten yet. I smell food, though, so maybe you have. Shoot." She looked like a doll when she pouted, all cute with her petite, freckled features perfectly frozen into place.

Rem shook his head. "Nope. Thomas got some food. That's what's in the trash, but I could eat."

"Great!" She grinned up at him, then shared the same genuinely happy expression with me. "Thomas, do you want to join us? There's plenty to eat in the food section of campus. They even have smoothies if you aren't that hungry anymore. Or they have chocolate chip cookies. I haven't tried them, but my roommate says they're delicious. She ate three this morning. I was so jealous."

I shook my head. I was extremely sure I would not be joining them. "No thanks. I think I'll go explore campus for a while. See you both later. Have fun." I really hoped they didn't want to go with me.

"Great. Well, bye, then," Rem said, ushering his girlfriend out of the room as if he couldn't wait to be away from me, which was fine since I really needed to get away from her. And him too, because seriously, what the fuck was he doing cheating on her as if it was no big thing?

I gave them a ten-minute head start so I hopefully wouldn't run into them at all, then left as well. I wasted some time at the bookstore, a little more in the library, then got some crackers out of a machine and gave most of them to the ducks. They weren't very good, but the ducks seemed to like them just fine.

Not more than two hours had passed before I found myself back in my dorm room. Thankfully I was alone this time, and I happily flopped onto my bed and pulled out my book. I was nearly done, only thirty pages from the end, when Rem came back in. He was alone, and he gave me a tentative smile as he locked the door behind himself.

"So...," he said as he went to his bed and took off his shoes.

I didn't look away from my book. "So."

"Thanks for not being an ass today."

I set my book aside so I could turn over and glare at him. "You mean about you cheating on your girlfriend? Who, by the way, seems pretty nice from the five minutes I spent with her. She even know you're bi?"

He quickly shook his head and folded his hands between his knees. "No. No one does. Just the guys I've been with occasionally. I don't ever see them again, though, and you're the first to even know my real name." He dragged his hands through his curls. "Shit."

I nodded. It was easy to agree with him on that note. "Why lie to her? Why cheat on her at all?"

He lay down too, just as I was, and we watched each other from across the room. "Angela's really sweet. And we've been together for five years now. She's in love with me and...." He frowned and looked away from me.

"And you what? Don't have the balls to tell her that you don't love her back?"

21

Rem shook his head, and he looked so sad I actually felt a bit sorry for him. But only a little bit. "I can't be out, not right now, and probably not ever. It'll ruin my football career, and yeah, most guys don't make it. But the coaches have said I've got a real shot here to get to the pros. I can't mess that up."

"So what's your plan, then? Date her until she gets tired of you?" I snapped at him.

He nodded. "Or wants to get married." He shrugged and flopped onto his back. "I've been hooking up with guys for years. It was never supposed to be complicated, and it wouldn't have been until you showed up. Fuck."

"Yeah. That's your issue. That I was here the next day. Your dirty little secret." I rolled my eyes and wanted to throw something at him. But the only thing I had that was handy was my book, and I didn't want my bookmark to fall out or for him to keep it from me when I wanted to read it again.

"Why are you so upset anyway?" Rem snapped at me. "You met her for like five minutes, maybe, and all of a sudden you're being protective of her or something? You and I had sex at a party, if you don't remember. I could have been anyone. I could have been married with a whole bunch of kids or something, and you wouldn't have known."

I chewed on my bottom lip for a bit because, yeah, he was right. Being mad at him for cheating on his girlfriend, when he'd cheated with me, was a bit weird. "Do you cheat on her with girls too?"

"Nope. Just guys. And only once in a while."

"Twice in twenty-four hours, more like," I reminded him.

His face pinched. "Yeah, well…." He looked away from me and sighed. "It's stupid, but I can't be in the same room as you and not want you in some way. I mean, hell, even right now if you'd let me, I'd fuck you."

Okay, so it was nice to be wanted and wanted in a big way apparently. I groaned as I started to think of some horrible, "really not supposed to happen" kind of idea. "Just sex, right? Nothing else?"

He turned his head to look at me, and I sat up on the edge of my bed. "Huh?" he asked me. He sat up too.

I shrugged, not really knowing what I was doing, or thinking. "I want you too. Even if you are a cheating bastard. And I think she should know, but I get why you wouldn't want to try to be the first out bi quarterback in the pros. I can't imagine that your career would do all that well after you came out."

"There would be no career," he said with a snicker.

I figured as much. "And this year is going to be hard as hell if I have to deny myself and worry about this every single time we're alone together. So just sex, we always use protection, and you don't cheat on her with any other guys?"

"You trying to negotiate with me?" he asked me with a wide smile.

No. I shook my head. I was trying to keep my sanity. Even now I wanted to go to my knees in front of him and take him back in my mouth. I'd thought having a sexy roommate I could mess around with would be fun. And it still could be, if I didn't worry about Angela and how hurt she'd probably be to find out that her boyfriend was sleeping around. "What do you say?"

He got off his bed and came over to me. We were kissing a moment later, with him bent over me. "Yeah. We can do that. Can I suck you off now? I've wanted to since you swallowed me this morning."

I was already undoing my pants and pushing them down my hips. "Yes. Please." I lay back on my bed, and he helped me get my pants off. His mouth was warm and wet around my head, and he wasted no time sucking me down. I put one hand in his hair, just touching him, and leaned back against the pillow. If he didn't care that he was cheating on Angela, I shouldn't either. That was a comforting thought, in a way, and the great feeling of him taking me in all the way helped chase away any lingering doubt.

He bobbed his head over my cock, moaning softly as he went, and I trembled under him. I'd been blown before, plenty of times, but having Rem's mouth on me was somehow different. Like it meant more since we'd had sex. Since he'd been my first. Maybe also

23

because we were living together, and if he hadn't been dating Angela, we might have been able to have a real relationship.

Nope. Couldn't think about that. He tangled his fingers around my free hand. I sank into the bed with his weight above me and closed my eyes as I focused only on the feeling of his mouth around my head, his tongue running over the tip, and the soft sounds he made as he gave me pleasure.

He helped me put my legs over his shoulders. It was kind of new for me, but when he slid a finger inside of me, that was really new. I actually jumped. Just a little, though. I didn't want him to know I'd never been fingered before, unless when he'd been stretching me a little while we were both drunk the night before counted. I took my hand off his hair so I could cover my mouth. My moans grew louder each time he slid his finger in and out of me.

I came before I realized I was really close, and he drank me down.

"I want to fuck you," he told me as he pulled away from me. I nodded, still kind of overwhelmed from the heat of my climax and the feeling of having a finger inside me. He didn't pull off his jeans as he pushed me onto my side and climbed up my body. And I could still feel that stiff material against the backs of my thighs as he put a condom over his cock and replaced his fingers with his thick length.

He quickly brought his hand up to cover my mouth when I cried out. One hand on my hip, the other over my mouth, and him right behind me as he thrust into me on the bed. "Fuck, fuck, fuck," I mumbled, my voice garbled against his hand.

I felt his hot breaths against my shoulder, all the way through my shirt. He still had his clothes on too, and I whimpered through his fingers as he fit us together and ground against me.

"God you feel good, Thomas. Too fucking good," he moaned against my neck.

I nodded, knowing exactly what he meant. I'd been raised right, and I knew that cheating was wrong. But this felt too good to stop, too good to ignore, and I wanted everything from him. I needed it. I'd never been so overwhelmed with pleasure or felt so much like

I absolutely could not go another minute without touching another person, as I did with him.

He came in me and lingered next to me, his mouth against my neck, his fingers still on my hip. I paid attention to each sensation this time. I wasn't drunk, so I got to savor each beat of his cock inside of me, each little pulse, as he emptied himself into the condom.

I didn't realize I'd gotten hard again until he moved his hand that was on my hip to my base. With his hand still over my mouth and his cock still deep inside of me, he stroked me. I rubbed myself against him, needing so much more of him, as he slid his hand over my slick cock. It didn't take me long to come again. In fact, it was embarrassingly fast, but when I was done, he pulled out of me, turned me back over, then kissed me hard. I was sticky and really overheated, but he lay down on me, right between my legs, and kept kissing me like he didn't even care.

"Thanks," he said after a few minutes where he'd had his tongue shoved into my mouth. I nodded. Damn, he had pretty green eyes. "You're fun. I'm glad I got you as a roommate."

Rolling my eyes, I pushed him off me. "Yeah. Lucky you." He fell onto the floor with a laugh, and I got up. I grabbed one of my towels from the stack of them I'd made by the sink and went into the bathroom to get a shower.

The hot water helped me feel clean, and the time alone let me think. God, Rem was hot. Like, bend me over, not even caring about anything else, fuck me now please, kind of hot. Just thinking about him, not even in a sexual way either, made heat go straight to my cock. I shook my head and sighed loudly.

"Hey, you okay?"

I didn't even hear Rem come into the bathroom. "Yep. Supergood." He pulled back the shower curtain, and I rolled my eyes at him. "First day and already you're interrupting my showers?"

"Well, yeah." He shrugged. "So. You sure you're okay? Because, and we don't know each other at all, but you don't really sound like it, and I'm pretty sure you're one of those guys who might suck at lying when you're hurting. Just a guess, though."

I nodded. Maybe I was okay. Maybe I could be if he'd give me a minute to think. Hell. Maybe not. "I want you, but I don't want to hurt her. She seems nice. I don't know her, but she obviously seems to care about you. Maybe I just need a minute alone without wanting to fuck you."

He gave me a little smirk. "That bad for you too, huh?"

It really was pretty awful to feel like all my morals didn't matter and all I wanted was him, in any way that I could have him. "Yep. Same for you?"

"Yeah. Normally it's just about fucking and being done. But with you? Not so much. I just had you, and I want you again already." He looked as surprised by that as I felt. "Want to share the shower?"

Tempting. So very, very tempting. But no. I shook my head. "I need a minute alone. And if you come in here, not only will I not be alone, but we'll be having sex again for sure."

"You think so?" he teased me.

I rolled my eyes. I knew so. But if he wanted to play…. "The hot water flowing over us, me on my knees, your hands buried in my hair, my mouth over your cock, me taking you all the way in until—"

"Shit." He tossed up his hands. "Fine. Yeah. We need a second apart." He was gone a moment later, and I was left smiling at the closed door. Well, that was one way to get rid of him when I wanted to be alone, I figured. I had to remember that tactic.

CHAPTER FOUR

WHEN I got out of the shower, Angela was in our room again, and I was so very glad I'd thought to put a towel around me. "Hey," I said to them both while she sat there in Rem's arms and they watched something on the laptop.

Angela grinned at me. "Hey. You should totally see this video Rem found. This guy put a firecracker in his butt and lit it. He jumped like twenty feet in the air."

I snickered and shook my head. My clothes were in a tote under the bed, and I was careful to keep my towel wrapped around me as I crouched down to pull out a pair of shorts. "Sounds great. Give me one minute to get dressed, though."

"Okay." She wasn't even looking at me anymore. Instead her attention was solely focused on Rem, and I probably could have dropped the towel and put on my shorts right there while she was kissing him. I might have too, if I'd actually wanted to see his tongue in someone else's mouth. I turned away, rolled my eyes, then went back to the bathroom to put my shorts on. My dirty clothes went into my laundry basket, and I didn't bother putting on a shirt for Rem's benefit. Even in the dorms with the air conditioning going full blast around us, it was still so humid there. I didn't know how people lived in Miami full time. I was really looking forward to going back home on the first break I got.

I was deciding what I wanted to do, between staying in the room and making it awkward as they kept kissing, or going out and finding something to do for a while to be alone and try my best not to think about him, when Rem miraculously got his tongue out of his girlfriend's mouth.

He was blushing when he smiled at her, and when he glanced over at me, I was quick to look away. Knowing they were together and seeing him kiss her, were two completely different things. I pulled out my book and focused on the words as hard as I could.

"There's an ice cream social in the dorm tonight, with a movie too," Angela told him. "Want to come with me, babe? I think it might be nice to meet some new friends. We could mingle. I could show off my sexy football star boyfriend."

Rem laughed, and that sound sent heat straight down my belly to my dick, which definitely didn't need any more encouragement right then.

"Sure," Rem said. I heard them get off the bed and watched over the top of my book as he pulled a clean shirt out of the totes he'd shoved under his own bed, just like I had. It was green and nearly matched his eyes. I wanted him to fuck me while wearing it.

"That shirt is so pretty on you. I'm glad I found it and that you like to wear it," Angela said. They kissed again, and I nearly squinted at my book as I forced myself to take it in and not look at them or think about them or anything else that had anything to do with the man I wanted and his girlfriend. Fuck, I'd gotten myself into some crazy mess already.

"Thanks. Thomas, you want to come with us?" Rem asked me.

I looked away from my book to look up at him and forced a smile. "No thanks. I'm going to finish this book before the semester starts. Have fun."

At least Rem didn't ask me again or try to push me into coming with them. He just gave me a nod and said, "See you later," before taking Angela's hand. They were gone a moment later, and I got up to lock the door behind them.

"Fucking hell," I groaned as I went back to my bed. Getting Rem all to myself wasn't going to happen, so I either had to find a way to not have sex with him for an entire year of living with him, which wasn't going to happen, or get over him having a girlfriend somehow.

I pulled out my phone and started dialing my mom's number. I wasn't going to tell her about having sex with Rem, but I did need to hear a friendly voice. "Hey," I said as soon as someone picked up.

"Thomas?" I'd called the home number since my mom wasn't great about charging her cell phone, so I shouldn't have been all that surprised that their foster kid Dusty had answered the phone. He was six and probably going to live with his grandparents in Loveland in a month or two, once they got custody of him.

"Hey. How's things there?" Dusty wasn't my mom or even my dad, but he was a friendly voice, and I'd settle for that right then.

"Great! We caught a raccoon in a trap!"

"Did you now? Wow. I bet that was exciting." God I missed being at home.

"It was. You should have been here. It was all bitey and snarly. Like a monster."

It sounded horrible, and I was actually kind of glad I'd missed that, since I would have been the one to stay with it until animal control arrived to take it away. Ugh. No thank you. "Sounds like a lot of fun," I told him instead of what I'd actually been thinking. He was six. Rabid, wild animals that would have likely clawed his face off were probably the coolest thing in the world to him next to slime and poop. I was just guessing there, though. I'd grown up around lots of different kids, but it wasn't as if I actually planned to have any of my own, so what they liked and what they did when I wasn't responsible for watching them had never been all that big of a deal to me. "Hey, Dusty, I gotta go. I just wanted to check in on things there."

"Oh. Okay. Miss you, Thomas." The little kid sounded so disappointed, and maybe I should have stayed on the phone with him, but I needed to get off and go entertain myself for a while.

"Miss you too. Say hi to everyone for me."

"Okay."

He hung up first, and I put my phone down on the floor next to my bed where I could charge it. I could have gone out to explore the campus, but I decided to stay in for the night instead. I put on my own music, some slow rock, and ordered myself a pizza for dinner. My parents had given me a credit card for food and stuff I'd need while on campus, along with a strict warning not to spend too much. I knew that eating out every day wasn't going to be possible. But I didn't really want to go find food and risk running into Rem and Angela either.

My large pepperoni pizza arrived nearly an hour later, with an apology from the guy who had trouble finding my room. It wasn't all that big of a deal to me. I sat on my bed, turned on the little TV that had come with the room, and settled into a classic horror movie.

I was almost done and clutching my pillow tightly to my chest, when I heard the door slowly open behind me. I froze, waiting for a ghost to reach out and grab me like they were in the movie, but it was only Rem. "Mind if I turn the lights on?"

"Sure. Go ahead." He did, and I relaxed a little as yellow light flooded the room. "There's pizza. Help yourself." Though it was a few hours old by then.

I glanced over at him as he sat down on his bed with a slice of pizza in one hand. At least we were alone. "Things good here?" he asked me.

I nodded and went back to watching my movie instead of focusing on the pink lipstick mark on the side of his neck. "Yep. How was the mingling?"

"Good. I guess. If you like that sort of thing."

His voice told me that he didn't really, that he'd gone to make Angela happy, and I tried not to let that affect me in any way. But it made part of me glad that he liked hanging out with strangers just as little as I did. Another part of me was kind of annoyed that he'd done something just to please her when him staying with me would have been far more fun for us both.

But I realized a few seconds later it was stupid of me to not expect him to do things for her. They'd been together longer than

I'd known most of my friends. Of course he'd do things to make her happy, and I was a jerk for thinking otherwise.

"Pizza from your parents?" he asked me. "They do know that there are places to eat here right?"

I shot him a smile before I watched the kids in the movie walk in on the ghost feeding from their parents. Lots of screaming ensued, and I hoped no one in the rooms around us was trying to sleep. It was late evening, though, so I was pretty sure no one was going to be coming over to tell me to turn it down anytime soon. "Yeah, they know. I bought it. Didn't feel like going out." He didn't get to know why. It was enough that I'd shared just that much with him.

He nodded and finished off the slice. "Thanks for dinner, then."

"Sure."

My movie was over a half an hour later and ended with everyone dying. It was a Japanese horror movie, and those ghosts didn't play around and get reasoned with like the American ones seemed to. "That was a bit bleak," Rem said as I turned the TV to the news, then tossed him the remote so he could put whatever he wanted on.

I smiled at him and lay down on my side. "Yeah. That's one of the reasons I like it. We have the big orientation in the morning. Want to sit together?"

"You mind if Angela sits with us?"

I didn't really know why he was asking me that, since she was his girlfriend, so of course she would be there with us, but I shook my head *no* anyway. "Why would I?"

He shrugged and lay down just like I was. If we were sharing a bed, I could have cuddled with him. I could have just as easily gotten off my ass and gone over to lie down next to him, but if I got to touch him, that would make me want to do way more than just cuddle him. And I didn't really want to have sex with him when he had pink lipstick on his neck. So I stayed right where I was and was miserable because of it.

"She missed it, but I saw how uncomfortable you were when she was here," Rem said, calling me out on it.

"And you're completely fine with your girlfriend and the guy you're having sex with being in the same room? Because, yeah, I was a little weirded out. And damn she's nice. Like, seriously? She's adorable."

He rolled his eyes, but I did see him smile there just a little bit. "Hey, I'm figuring this out as I go here too. She is nice, though. Sometimes I wish I really did love her. Or that I wanted her as much as I want you all the time. She's sweet, and she's always been great to me. Her dad's this big government guy back in Tallahassee. He used to chaperone all of our dates up until she turned eighteen and became an adult in his eyes. When we were packing up to come here, he kept telling me about that old gun in his bedroom that he'd shine up and bring out just for me if I ever hurt his little girl."

I snickered and shook my head before rolling over onto my stomach. "Oh wow. My parents are nothing like that."

"No? What are they like, then?"

I shrugged, thinking about them back home in their little house that was always so cramped but never felt claustrophobic, like having a ton of people in it actually was how the house was supposed to be, and anything less than that just would not work for it or anyone in it.

"Mom works at the diner and Dad is a manager at the grocery store. He does construction sometimes on the side too, if someone needs a deck fixed or their toilet isn't working anymore. It's more of a handyman thing, but my dad calls it construction. Mom found me my first date when I was thirteen. He was fourteen, and we saw him at a mall about half an hour from home. Dad gave me condoms as soon as he found a muscle magazine in my room. Told me to be safe and have fun. They're...." I struggled to find a word that would sum up my completely casual, absolutely trusting parents. "Really great." Lame, yes, but it fit them. I thought they were perfect.

Rem was staring at me, though. "They don't care that you're gay?"

I shook my head. "Nope. Not at all. It's a tiny town, and I know everyone in it. And I've heard that some tiny towns are awful for gay guys, but it's the kind of place where if you don't go around shooting at the neighbor's cattle or running your ATV through their yard, then they won't really care what else you're doing." I had the sudden urge to drag Rem back home with me over fall break, to have him meet my parents, and take him on the ATV trails that ran along the outskirts of town. They were mostly for hunters, but I'd grown up using them well before Dad had taught me how to hold his rifle. Even before I'd finished the thought, though, I realized that wouldn't be happening. He and Angela probably went somewhere together during their breaks, or they would be now that they were in college and could take trips. Even if we were just friends and pretended to be nothing more, he'd probably never go away with me.

"Sounds nice."

I nodded. "It is." I looked over at him, and I couldn't help looking at the lipstick he still had on his neck. Did he just not realize Angela had left her mark on him, claiming him for all the world—and, it seemed, especially me—to see? Of course she couldn't know what I'd done with her boyfriend, or what he'd done to me. Repeatedly. But it sure felt like she was planting a shiny Angela-shaped flag right there on the side of his neck.

"A lot different than at home," he continued, as if he couldn't tell I was staring at him.

"Did you intend to cheat on her? The first time I mean?" I found myself asking him, despite the fact that I really shouldn't have, and that I didn't really want to know. Not really anyway. Okay, so maybe I did want to know a little.

He frowned over at me. "Huh? Where'd that come from?"

I nodded over to his neck. "You have lipstick on you." I didn't say where it was, but when he lifted up his shirt and looked down his stomach, I was pretty sure I should have been more specific. "On your neck. Seriously?" I was annoyed at him and at me for caring. And stupidly at her for going down on him too.

He sat up, with his hand cupped around the lipstick mark on his neck and gave me a sheepish grin. "I'll be right back after I wash this off."

"Uh-huh."

It still wasn't all that late, but I'd had kind of a train wreck of a day in some ways, so getting under my big blue blanket, one I'd loved since I was fifteen and had gotten for a birthday present, sounded like a great idea to me. I was under it with the fluffy blanket pulled up to my shoulders when he came back from the sink.

"All better?" he asked me as he leaned over me.

I nodded, and since he was close enough for me to touch, I did. I pressed my fingertips to the side of his neck, where he'd scrubbed himself red, and when he leaned down to kiss me, I didn't push him away.

He kissed my lips, my cheek, then placed a quick kiss on my nose before he stepped away from me again. I didn't try to stop him. Truthfully I needed the distance from him for a few seconds. Kissing him reminded me of sex, and I needed not to think about that right now. "So tell me about the first time."

Rem sat back down on his bed, and like me, he got under his blanket as he got comfortable. His was black and a lot thicker than mine. I wondered how he'd be able to sleep with that much heat around him and the heavy humidity in the air. I was sure I was going to be taking my blanket off in a little bit, but I liked having it on me right now. "The first time I cheated on her, you mean?"

I nodded. Exactly that. "Did you mean to? Or was it an accident that you found out you liked guys, and it went on from there?"

"You make me sound like a horrible person for cheating on her," Rem said with a frown.

I didn't deny that, and eventually he sighed. "I can't help that I'm attracted to both men and women."

Now that really wasn't an excuse, and I was more than ready to call him out on that kind of bullshit. "Plenty of bi people never cheat. That's a myth that you all are more prone to cheating. All it means is that if you wanted to cheat, you have more options, so don't even think that excuses what you've done."

He rolled his eyes. "And what about what you've done? It's not like you've ever pushed me away. You know I'm with her, and you still let me touch you, let me kiss you. I've seen you naked with water running down your body even after you knew I was with her, so don't make this all about me and have it be all one-sided."

"Yeah, I can't resist you. I think that's been made pretty fucking clear by now. But you're the one in the relationship with her, not me, so it's your responsibility not to cheat, not mine for not being able to tell you no when you're so goddamn tempting all the time."

There was only silence to my words as Rem chewed on his bottom lip and stared up at the ceiling. "You're right."

"I know."

He smirked a little as he turned back to me. "You don't have to be a jackass about it."

Shrugging, I waited for him to come up with an explanation I might have believed. There wasn't going to be one, I was pretty sure of that, but I still wanted him to put forth some kind of an effort to explain what he'd been thinking the first time he cheated on her.

"I was at a party in high school. She couldn't go out, but I wanted to go anyway. It was a few towns over, and I wanted to see what the football competition was going to be like. I kissed a guy for the first time there, and I wasn't drunk or anything, so I couldn't even blame it on that."

"And then what?"

He gave me a sad little smile and propped his chin on his fist as he looked over at me. "Then… I dunno. I couldn't stop thinking about that kiss. It wasn't so much him, just more the feeling of him kissing me. Of being gripped by someone that was actually stronger than me, of a little bit of stubble touching me. It was so different than kissing Angela was, but they were both good ways of kissing in their own rights. I just wanted to have them. I'd thought about guys before, off and on, but mostly as a passing curiosity, and that kiss kind of changed things for me."

It wasn't how I'd started. Not anything close to it, since I'd always known I was gay and had never questioned it since the first time I'd tried to kiss a boy in school when I was six. My parents had been far more upset that I'd gotten suspended for the kiss rather than that I'd actually tried to kiss him. His parents hadn't been so forgiving of my innocent gesture.

"Do you ever think of just not cheating on her?" It was a legitimate question, but I didn't really think he'd have a good answer for it.

He shrugged. "If you absolutely, 100 percent, had to be straight, could you do it?"

For me the answer to his question was easy. "Hell no. So even if you were with a guy, you'd still cheat on him with a girl? Or what?"

He frowned over at me and let out a giant sigh before answering me. "I don't know. The only thing I'm absolutely sure of is that I can't stop thinking about you, even though I've only known you for twenty-four hours."

After he told me that, I went quiet as I lay there in my bed looking up at the ceiling. Eventually I turned away from him and stared at the wall.

CHAPTER FIVE

HE QUIETLY went to bed about an hour after that, but I was still up at two. I turned over and watched him sleeping. I wasn't being creepy or anything like that. It was more that I liked looking at him. Which, okay, maybe was a bit creepy actually. And maybe if I watched him long enough, I could get over my fucking need to get my ass out of bed and join him in his. I didn't want to have sex, but I was pretty sure if I did touch him, it would lead to kissing, which would end up with us having sex again.

"What's wrong?" he asked me around four when I was still wide-awake and he got up for some water.

I shrugged. "Can't sleep."

"Because I snore?" He came back and put the glass of water next to his bed before he climbed back in.

Shaking my head, I sat up, same as him, as we looked at each other across the room. "Just… I like you too. And I want you all the time. It's never been like this for me, and I wish you weren't with her and that we'd somehow have a real chance."

I could see his sad little smile, even in the near darkness of our room with only the hall light shining in through the crack under the door. "We wouldn't, though, even if she wasn't in the picture. Because I can't be out. But I know what you mean."

And there it was, the truth of it. Even if I had him to myself, I couldn't ever actually be with him. No holding hands between the palm trees, no kissing on the beach. I'd be just his secret, someone to spend time with where the rest of the world couldn't see us. And that would never be good enough for me. "I'm going to ask for a room change after orientation tomorrow."

"What are you going to say for your reason?" He sounded resigned, like he knew that was the best thing for both of us. It was easy to actually get a clear thought out when he wasn't close enough to touch.

I shrugged. I hadn't given it much, if any thought actually. I'd really just decided a few seconds before that I was going to talk to the dorm guy and see if I couldn't be moved. "That I want someone who isn't straight." It was a lie because really I only wanted him. But maybe I'd get some cute gay guy and he would be just as hot and make me want him just as much. Even as I thought it, I realized the chances of me completely wanting someone else this much was going to be slim to none. It was like Rem had somehow put himself under my skin, and now I couldn't help wanting him, needing him every single second that I was awake. Even when I'd just finished with him, I still had to be close to him, to feel him touching me. It was like I couldn't get enough of him, and we'd only known each other a day.

He nodded and started getting back under the covers. "Thanks."

"For what?"

Rem turned to look back at me when he'd pulled his blanket back up under his arms. "For trying to find a way to make this easier on us both. If they do move you, would you like to try to be friends still?"

"Friends who don't have sex?"

He nodded, and I shrugged. I didn't know if I could be that for him. "Maybe." By that point I was completely awake, and trying to go back to sleep was probably going to be hopeless. I was pretty sure of it anyway. So I got out of bed and then pulled my hoodie out of a tote under my bed.

"Where are you going?" he asked as I yanked it on before putting my feet into my sneakers.

"For a walk, I guess. I'll be back in a while."

He nodded, and I headed out as quietly as I could. Walking around campus without anyone else around was a bit creepy, so it didn't take me long to head to the water. With it only a few blocks away from campus, I knew I would have been there sooner or later. I'd thought it would have been during the day, though, with the sun shining on me and me being able to casually stare at guys running around without shirts on. Instead there was only one guy, and he passed me silently in the gray dawn as he ran down the beach.

I wasn't there to run, not that I was all that good at it anyway, so I sat down in a spot that was fairly dry and looked out at the nearly black surf. Being from Colorado, the ocean had only been this thing in movies and pictures to me. Seeing it in person and getting to smell the salty sea air as it blew against my face made me think maybe my issues with Rem weren't all that big of a deal. Maybe I didn't need to move out, and we could just be friends.

I stayed there for a long time, though how long I couldn't say for sure. I'd forgotten my phone, and even if I'd had it with me, I had no idea when I'd left the dorm. When the sun was fully up, though, and I heard cars rushing on the streets behind me, I figured I had to start heading back to my room. I had orientation this morning and really hoped I'd left myself enough time to be able to get a shower before I had to be down there.

The beach was a lot more crowded now with people jogging, some walking their dogs, and parents with their kids in funky wrap things that left their hands free to hold more little hands. I smiled at one mom with a whole pack of wild kids as I got up and headed toward the water. I expected it to taste like salt when I cupped a little and brought it to my lips for a drink, which it did, but it wasn't the kind of salt that Mom had made me swish with when I had my wisdom teeth out. I made sure to remember the feeling of it on my tongue, how it was almost heavy, so I could tell my mom about it later.

By the time I got back to the dorms, people were walking around, but at least Rem was still there, so I couldn't have been all that late. "How long do I have until orientation?" I asked him as I stripped off my hoodie. Angela was there already, and I had a moment to be self-conscious before I remembered the orientation was mandatory and I needed to get moving if I was going to get a shower.

"Fifteen minutes. Want us to wait for you? We could walk down together," Rem offered.

I nodded. "Yeah, if you wouldn't mind." I didn't wait for his answer as I grabbed some shorts and a T-shirt from a tote and headed into the shower. I was in and out in record time, dressed, and with my hair marginally better before they got up to head to the door. I brushed my teeth in a hurry as Rem unlocked it, and he only had to give me one pointed look before I was out with them and we were headed to orientation. Thank God they knew where to go because I had no idea.

"Hey, you okay?" I asked Angela when we'd found a table to sit at near the back.

She gave me a little nod, then looked to Rem. She was sitting between us because I'd made sure to put her there, and now that I looked at him too, he looked a little sad as well. "Yeah," she said, giving me a little smile. "Well, actually, not really. My roommate said something this morning that weirded me out a little."

"Okay…." I looked over to Rem to see if he knew what she was talking about, but he looked as clueless as I felt. "What'd she say?"

Angela shifted in her seat, and her smile got a little brighter, but like she was forcing it out. "She said that I shouldn't spend so much time in your guys' dorm, that it was rude. Only I don't really want Rem in my dorm. I have a pic of us framed and up on my side of the room, and she keeps talking about how hot he is and what she'd do to him if she was his girlfriend. It's weird."

"Ew. Okay, that's creepy." I shuddered. "You're fine. Come over whenever, even when he's not there. We can watch TV or something. Like studying." She gave me a big smile that was real this time, and it was hard not to think about how pretty she was when she was really happy. She gave my arm a big hug, and I met Rem's gaze over her head. He looked surprised, and if he'd been alone when I'd come in, then he would have gotten an explanation. But this was good too. I liked being able to throw him off his game. And telling her she could come over whenever didn't sting as much as I thought it would.

"Thank you, Thomas," she practically squealed as she kept hugging me.

"Sure thing."

Orientation went smoothly after that, with Angela being much more like her perky self, and at the end of it, she went off with her friends, and Rem and I walked back to our dorm room in silence. As soon as we were behind the closed door, that changed, though.

"What was that about?" he asked.

I shrugged and stripped off my shirt to get more comfortable in the sticky, hot room. "What part? Where I tried to make nice with your girlfriend?"

He laughed, and we sat down on our beds across from each other. "More like where you made her feel comfortable and happy at the same time. It was big of you. Thanks for that."

"At the beach this morning, I decided that I'd rather try to be your friend, and maybe even hers, than fight this all the time. I may still screw up once in a while and be unable to resist you, but I don't want to see if they'll let me move." It wasn't an absolute solution, especially with him looking at me like I'd just made his whole week, but I figured that I could give it a try.

"And I promise not to jump on top of you all the time and make it hard for you to say no," he promised me with a grin.

I rolled my eyes, and things were okay between us for a bit. Wanting him was a constant, but I could always go take a shower when it got to be too hard to ignore the need to have him. We made it a whole two days like that. Granted, we were tiptoeing around each other, but we still made it.

I had to get through my one language class to get the credits, and I'd never been all that good at languages, so I decided to get a head start on it. Mom and Dad had suggested Spanish because it was supposed to be easy or something, but really it wasn't easy at all.

I lay on my bed, staring at my book and trying to figure out what the hell *vosotros* meant or how a word could have a gender, when I just shook my head and groaned.

"You look like you're miserable, and the semester hasn't even started yet," Rem joked with me from where he was drinking one of his protein drinks and sitting on the counter in what was kind of our kitchen. Closest thing we had to it anyway.

Shrugging, I looked up at him. We'd made it through an entire two days without having sex, and yeah, it kind of really sucked. I'd nearly gotten up in the middle of the night to join him in his bed about five times last night. Maybe my lack of sleep was the cause of me not being able to concentrate on this book.

"I'm trying to seem like I actually know something before I get to Spanish class on Monday," I told him with a sigh.

He laughed and kept drinking something that was supposed to be chocolate. I loved chocolate, but even I wasn't desperate enough to get my chocolate fix to drink one of those things. "Read me something."

"Huh?" I asked him.

He shrugged and leaned forward over his knees. "Let's see what they've got you learning in this most basic of Spanish classes. Read me something."

"Okay…." I turned to a random page and read. "*Una mujer bebe el…* er… *una… agua…* and stuff." I stopped reading and looked up at him instead, only to find him smiling at me and looking damn irresistible. "I'm going to fail this class. I'm sure of it. I've always been horrible with languages."

Laughing, he shook his head and jumped down from the counter. I froze as he lay down on top of me after tossing his drink in the trash. "Um. What are you doing?"

"Helping you." He put one arm under my chest then rested his chin on my shoulder. I could see him out of the corner of my eye, but more than that I could feel him rubbing against me. If he expected me to actually learn something here, he was a lot more confident about it than I was. He pulled my book close and turned it to the first lesson. "There we go. *La mujer bebe agua.* The woman drinks water. *Las mujeres beben agua.* So where we say 'the women drink water,' they use *beben* instead of drink."

I nodded. Okay, so that might make sense. "What level Spanish are you in?"

"Five. But only because I'm fluent. My grandmother is from Spain."

I laughed and ignored how warm he was making me. "Great. So you'll do my Spanish homework for me, right?"

Biting his lip, I saw him grin and knew what he was thinking because right away I was thinking the same thing. "What will you give me if I do?"

I shrugged. "What do you want?"

He leaned in close to my ear, nearly pressing his mouth to my lobe, and I shivered. "*Quiero tener sexo contigo aquí y ahora.*"

"What…." I licked my lips. "What does that mean?"

Instead of answering me, he rubbed against me, dipping his hips against my ass. "What do you think it means?"

"That your grandmother taught you some naughty phrases. And that my Spanish lesson is over for the day." I reached under me to start pushing down my pants. I'd worn ones with elastic to make it easier for him to get to me, in the hopes that we would get to this place again. It didn't even bother me that I had picked out what clothes I'd be wearing for the day based on how much I wanted to have sex with him.

He gave me a big sloppy kiss on my temple. "Right on one at least." With my pants out of the way, he gave my butt a hard squeeze. "Tell me to stop this and I will."

He might have been a good guy for giving me that offer, but I was no saint, and not being able to touch him for two days had left me nearly desperate and my cock practically raw from jacking myself off. "I want you."

He nodded, his rough stubble rubbing against the side of my face and making me shiver under him. I was stretched, prepped for him in no time at all, and when he slid into me, the pain and pressure mixed together and made me groan so loudly he clamped his hand over my mouth to keep me quiet.

I tried not to think about Angela, about how sweet she was or how she'd brought me a chocolate chip cookie and told me not to share it with Rem after I'd told her she could come over all the time. I didn't want to think about how much knowing I was having sex with Rem would hurt her, and so I pushed her out of my mind the best I could. It was easier, once the pleasure of having him inside me took over, and once he brought his nails to my hip and squeezed me hard enough to leave bruises, I'd nearly forgotten about her.

I came with short grunts against his hand as I rubbed myself onto my sheets. He jerked against me, his thrusts becoming erratic enough that any rhythm he'd had was completely gone by the time he came. Using a condom meant that he was pretty clean, but I had to do laundry if I wanted to have a sheet to sleep on that night. We were silent as he kissed me and wrapped himself around my body, our legs rubbing against each other. This would have been so much easier if the warmth and happiness I felt after coming with him was how it could be all the time, if I never had to give the after-sex Rem that I saw back to the world.

He gave me a gentle kiss and sucked on my bottom lip before getting up. "I'm going to take a shower. Angela will be over in about an hour."

He might not have been implying that I needed to get cleaned up and look a lot less like I'd just had sex, but that's how I took it. "I'll be ready."

Rem smiled at me. "Thanks."

There was time for me to get the sheet into the washer and for us to have two completely separate showers, as much as I wanted to join him in his before she came over. If Angela thought it was weird that I didn't have a sheet on my bed or that we both had wet hair, she didn't mention it as we all sat down to watch TV together.

CHAPTER SIX

CLASS WAS.... Okay, class was boring. But it was only the first week, so really it was just a lot of procedures and policy stuff, and I was fairly certain it would get more interesting. At least I hoped it did because I'd nearly fallen asleep during Intro to Chemistry. Spanish, surprise surprise, wasn't all that boring, but that was mostly because I'd been thinking about Rem's voice in my ear, his weight on top of me, his scruff against my cheek as he screwed me.

Not the best way to focus in class, but it had worked, so I wasn't going to be one to really judge. I was, however, extremely excited to hear someone in front of our dorm room door since I hadn't seen Rem since that morning when he'd gone off to his classes, and I'd gone off to mine.

Only Rem had a key, and this person knocked. My hopes were dashed immediately. "Hey," I told Angela as I opened the door and saw her standing there. "Rem's not here right now."

She bit her bottom lip and struck her cutest pose that was somewhere between adorably pouty and cheerleader perfect. "I know. It's just... my roommate's got her boyfriend over, and he's kind of a pain... and remember last week when you said I could come stay here even when Rem wasn't here sometimes if I wanted to? I was wondering if maybe you wanted to hang out for a bit. Rem won't be done with football practice for another hour...." She was looking more deflated by the second.

It would be a good thing to have her around, I decided. It would, at the very least, remind me that Rem was hers, and I needed to get better about the no sex thing. Four days without his naked body against me was nearly killing me. "Sure. Come on in. You hungry? I could order us something."

"Thanks. That would be great." She came in and put her messenger bag on the counter, and I pulled out my phone to get to the menus. "I'm not sure what I'd want. I mean, there's plenty of stuff I love, but for some reason lately it's been tasting a little weird. Like my taste buds are off or something. Maybe I'm getting a cold…." She shrugged and took up a spot on Rem's bed. We needed to get a few chairs or something in here so she could sit with us and we wouldn't have to awkwardly be on the beds Rem and I had already had sex on.

I swiped through the menus I'd saved to my phone as I looked at the choices. "Chinese, Thai, Sushi, Italian, subs, pizza, um… burgers?"

She chewed on her bottom lip a little. "Anything good for dessert? Don't worry about price. Not that I think you're poor or anything. In case you were wondering. I just… I want to treat you since you've been so nice to me. Letting me hang out here and all."

Shrugging, I kept going through my phone. Dessert was fine; so was letting her stay here. And I didn't even care that she might have thought I was poorer than her. The only thing I wanted from her was her boyfriend, and that wasn't going to be happening anytime soon. "Ice cream cookie sandwiches or cheesecake?" I asked her.

"Hmm. Both?"

Smiling, I ordered both of them, and when she handed me her credit card, I typed the numbers in. "Thirty minutes to a sugar rush."

"Great!"

We settled in to watch TV with her on Rem's bed and me sitting on mine. She was stretched out, looking completely relaxed and like she belonged there. She did, though, I reminded myself. She belonged in Rem's life in a way I didn't, that I couldn't be.

Rem got in an hour later and found me leaning over the counter in the kitchen nibbling on some cheesecake we had left. "Hey," he said, coming up behind me after I'd given him a little wave. I had cheesecake in my mouth and couldn't really say hi without showing him my food and being rude. Angela was in the bathroom so I wasn't surprised he didn't realize she was there and put his hand on my hip.

I was quick to swallow the cheesecake and smack his hand away. "Angela will be glad you're back early. Though you smell really horrible so you might want to take a shower before you hug her or something." I spoke loudly enough that Angela could hear me, just in case she thought we might be whispering or something.

Rem let go of me quickly and went slightly pale. "I see you got cheesecake," he said, just as loudly as I had. I got up on the counter and continued to eat the last of the cheesecake. Angela had said she'd had enough so I wasn't concerned about having to share it with her.

"Angela wanted it. We ordered pizza too. There's some left if you want any."

Angela came out of the bathroom, and I watched as they hugged and then kissed. "You need to shave. Your hair tickles," she said with a laugh. I liked his scruff, liked how it felt against my cheek when he was inside of me. And I liked feeling just that little bit of roughness against my lips when I kissed his cheek. I couldn't say any of that.

He really should have showered before coming back to the dorm because he smelled rank. "I'm going to go shower. I'll shave while I'm in there," he told Angela.

They kissed again, and I suddenly didn't want any more of the cheesecake. I slid off the counter, tossed the rest in the trashcan, and grabbed my hoodie. "I'm going to head out for a walk. See you two later."

Rem gave me a look over her head. Maybe it was that he didn't want me to go, maybe telling me that I didn't have to go. But really I was good. Going out for a walk would be good for me, and besides, I really didn't want to see them kissing and cuddling all night.

"Thanks for letting me hang out here," Angela told me.

I gave her a quick smile as I shoved my feet into my flip-flops. "Sure. Anytime." I meant it too. She was nice, and it wasn't her fault that I was falling for her boyfriend.

Going outside helped some. It wasn't all that late out, and there were people still walking around campus. I wished I'd thought to bring my laptop or something so I could hang out at the library and read. I wasn't in the mood to study, but I could have brought a new book and hung out there.

Instead I found myself on the beach again with the wind from the surf blowing through my hair. I checked my e-mails on my phone, which were nothing too important, and sat out there for a while. Mom and Dad missed me. Dusty won a spelling bee, and the brothers had already been placed with their grandmother. The baby was still a handful, but most babies were, and my mom seemed to be laughing off his antics and 1:00 a.m. tantrums. I shook my head as I read that. I liked kids, but I wasn't a saint like my mom was, and I didn't know if I would have been able to handle it all as well as she did.

After living next to the ocean for a while like I had, the newness and wonder of it had worn off in light of everything else in my life; it didn't hold quite the same mystery and excitement for me as it did when I'd first come to see it, and I found myself growing bored fairly quickly. Though that might have been because I couldn't stop thinking about Rem, and of course how Angela was probably currently wrapped around him. How they could hold hands in public. No, how he would hold hands in public with *her*. How he'd kiss her in the sunlight where anyone could see, how he'd hug her after a bad score on a test. I'd seen it, and I'd wanted it for myself.

I wasn't falling for a straight guy, but maybe this was even worse than that. Maybe it would be better if Rem was straight because then I wouldn't know what it felt like to kiss him, to hug him when it was just us and no one in the world could see. I wouldn't know what it was like to care about him so much I lay awake at night just thinking about how great it would be to be able to have him as only mine when he was lying not ten feet away from me.

Angry now, I threw a seashell back into the water, but it did nothing to make me feel better. It just sank with a loud plop into the surf, and I turned away from it. I went back to the dorm and had every intention of going into our room, even if Angela was still there, but once I got close enough, I heard Rem's bed squeaking, even through the door, and Angela wasn't quiet at all, not like I was when I was with him.

I felt sick wanting someone so much when he clearly wanted someone else, something else, more than he would ever want me. Wandering around some more let me find a horror movie club, and I sank into an open chair to waste away the next few hours as they played old horror movies and discussed them.

It was nearly midnight when I got back to the dorm. Exhausted and still annoyed, I decided I wouldn't care if she was still there, even if it was past curfew. She wasn't, but Rem was up waiting for me. At least that's what it looked like as he sat there on his bed, facing the doorway as I came through.

"Hi." I kicked off my flip-flops, shed my hoodie, and made sure Angela's bag wasn't anywhere around before I lay down on my bed. I rolled away from him, facing the wall, and hoped he wouldn't say anything.

I wasn't so lucky.

"You were gone a long time."

Shrugging, I didn't turn back to him. "I came back a few hours ago, but you were busy, so I found something else to do."

"I was busy? When?"

I wasn't in the mood for him to play stupid, so I turned over to face him and gave him my worst glare. "Maybe you should cover your girlfriend's mouth while you're fucking her too. Or is it okay for everyone to know that you're having sex with her?" Of course it was. He was the perfect straight quarterback for the Miami College Crusaders. They'd even made him first string. I shook my head and hated how much I still wanted him, even after knowing he'd had his dick in her just a few hours before.

I stormed into the bathroom and turned the shower on full blast. I'd need the heat to feel better. Rem didn't knock as he came into the bathroom with me, and I didn't try to hide the fact that I was naked from him. "I'm sorry," he said over the sound of the shower.

49

I shrugged. "There's nothing for you to be sorry about. This is my issue. You just keep doing what you're doing."

He pushed the curtain aside, and I glared at him. He shook his head and reached for me, but I moved away from him, just out of his reach. "I don't like that you're upset over this. What can I do?"

The way he said it, like it was my fault I was having trouble with him being with both of us at the same time made me laugh. "You could break up with her and actually come out." We both knew that was never going to happen, and I saw his face fall even as I said the words.

"Thomas…."

"No. Don't worry about it. I know that's not an option." I stepped into the shower, eager to get away from him for the moment but not really wanting to leave him either. Under the spray I watched him strip off his clothes and sighed as my cock started to harden at the sight of him.

I shook my head when he joined me in the shower. "I want you, but I don't want to have sex with you after you've just been with her." Even as I said it, I was backing up, making room for him under the shower's spray with me.

He reached for me, but I pushed his hand away. "Thomas, c'mon, just let me touch you. Please? Let me make this up to you."

I ran my hands through my wet hair and closed my eyes. This time when he ran his hands down my stomach, I didn't stop him or even try to push him away. I didn't feel like doing anything sexual with him, but thankfully I'd gotten the wrong idea. He folded me into his arms, and I laid my cheek against his shoulder. It was nice standing there in his arms with the hot water coming down over us, but it wasn't perfect by any means.

"This isn't working out," I told him as I lifted my hands from my sides to lay them over the small of his back.

He kissed my temple, then my cheek, and I felt him grow hard between us. "Give me another chance. Skip your classes tomorrow. Hang out with me instead. We'll get away from this place, just the two of us. Say yes. Say you'll spend the day with me."

"You have practice," I reminded him. We could skip our classes. That should have been a bigger deal to me than it really was.

Rem moved me back against the wall and pressed his mouth to mine. He brought his hands to my hips, then to my cock. I was hard. It was nearly impossible not to be when he was naked in front of me, but I still didn't want to have sex with him. Instead of asking me to, he simply ran his hands over me, gently giving me pleasure.

I closed my eyes and gave into his kisses and the feeling of having him holding me. It wasn't everything I wanted. Or even a little bit. But it was something. I came with his hand wrapped tightly around me and his mouth against my lips. If he were mine, this would have been everything I'd ever wanted. But he wasn't, and I couldn't pretend that our stolen moments were enough for me. But if they were all we had, then I'd make the most of them.

"Please be okay with this," Rem whispered to me later that night as we lay together on his bed with our arms around each other with the TV on in the background, though neither of us was watching it.

"I wish you'd tell her. She'll break up with you, but you don't love her anyway." I knew how useless it was to ask him that and how I was mostly just listening to myself talk at that point, but one of these times when I asked him to leave her, I wanted him to say yes. I was pretty sure he never would, though.

Rem shook his head and kissed my temple, though it did nothing to make me feel any better about the situation we'd found ourselves in. "I can't. I'll be going to the pros. I'll have sponsors, and my coach says that teams and sponsors look for a guy who shows real commitment and morals. Marrying my high school sweetheart will get that for me."

"You sound like a fucking infomercial," I snapped as I rolled away from him and went back to my own bed. So few guys went pro, and he knew that, so I didn't need to say there was a very real chance he wouldn't be one of them. I was sure he knew his chances and the statistics that said the odds were against him. But I cared about him too damn much to lash out at him any more than I already had.

I went to bed, covered myself up with my blanket, and hoped he didn't want to talk at all the rest of the night. I got my wish, and he left me alone. Even though I'd gotten exactly what I wanted, I still felt completely miserable as I lay there alone in my own bed with the person I absolutely cared about not more than ten feet from me and being unable to let myself get close to him. Because I knew what would happen if I did, and I didn't want to be hurt anymore.

Rem was up before I'd stopped pretending I was still asleep the next morning. Or that I'd gotten any sleep at all actually. He showered and had one of those disgusting protein shakes before he came over and shook me awake.

"I'm not asleep," I told him when he went from just rubbing my shoulder to get me up to putting his mouth on my earlobe, teasing me out of my inactivity.

He smiled as I turned over to face him. "I knew you weren't. You snore a little when you're actually asleep."

Frowning, I shook my head. "I do not."

"Sure you don't. Did you want to hang out with me today? Just the two of us?"

God he was tempting when he smiled at me like I was the most important person in his world. It was a lie, but it was a nice one to believe. "Yeah. Let's do that. I'll go get showered."

"I could join you."

I knew what he was hinting at, but it was fun to pretend for a second that I was a lot denser than I was. "You already had a shower, though."

He reached for me, and I let our hands come together as if I had no control over them at all. "Let me join you?" he asked me.

I considered his offer, thought about it pretty long and hard actually. But in the end, I shook my head. "Give me five minutes? I won't take long."

"Hurry up. I want to take you to this pier nearby with these games and the best funnel cake you've ever had."

Laughing, I grabbed up a towel. "That won't be hard since I've never had it."

"You poor deprived man." We were both laughing after that, and I hurried to get showered and dressed. I should have somehow known that wouldn't be what would happen that day, though. That day when everything changed.

Angela was in our room when I got out, and I ducked back into the bathroom to change before she saw me. I'd come out naked and hoping we could have a little fun before we went off on our adventure away from classes. I wasn't ready to give him all of me again while I was hurting so much, but I would have sucked him for sure.

Only Angela had been crying when I'd come out of the shower. And she was still crying when I came back out. Rem wasn't crying, so it couldn't have been something too awful, I told myself. But he didn't exactly look normal either as he sat there on his bed with this god-awful blank expression on his face.

"Rem?" I asked him. I should have tried to see if Angela was okay too, but she was crying so I figured she was dealing with whatever it was. Rem just looked shocked.

Angela gave me a hug, which I had no way to deal with. Not when I was trying to figure out what was going on with Rem. "What's wrong?" I asked her.

"I'm... I'm pregnant," she sobbed against my chest. And that was the moment when my world came crashing down. I sat down with her on Rem's bed, and she transferred her sobbing self over to Rem's chest. I watched as he wrapped his arms around her and laid his chin over her head. He looked just like he was protecting her from the rest of the world, like he'd always be there for her. And I knew he would.

I was sure they'd get married now and raise the baby together and live the perfect white-picket-pro-football kind of life. She had him, and he'd have everything he'd ever wanted. And I'd be forgotten so easily. It made me sick how easily I turned this into something about me, but I couldn't stop feeling that way.

Rem's gaze focused on me for a moment, and I saw how frightened he was. I didn't blame him in the least. I would have been terrified too. Angela's sobbing quieted, and she wiped roughly at her eyes. "Thanks for the hug, Thomas. You're such a great guy friend. The perfect kind." She sniffled, and her voice cracked. And I felt like she'd have done better just hitting me in the stomach.

I wasn't a good friend to her at all. I wanted her boyfriend for myself. I wanted him to be gay, not bi. And I wanted her to not be pregnant at all. I wanted the moments before I'd gone to take a shower back. I wanted to tell Rem he could join me in there. I wanted to have him to myself one last time because I could already clearly see the life they'd have together, the three of them. Or maybe more.

"It'll be okay," he told her. I wished someone would say that to me too, and somehow make me actually believe it was true, because I felt like I was breaking apart as well.

Angela hung out with us for the rest of the day, crying off and on, until curfew came and she had to go back to her own dorm. That left just Rem and me, sitting there on his bed, staring at the wall across from us.

"What are you going to do?" I asked him, even though I'd already realized he'd probably have a whole horde of babies with Angela someday and a big house to put them all in.

Rem shrugged and slipped his hand into mine. I was surprised by the contact, but I didn't pull away. I just settled my hand against his and waited for him to say something, anything. "What would you do?" he finally asked me.

Not have had sex with a girl for starters, I wanted to say. But I didn't want to hurt him. He was already pretty broken looking. "Adoption is an option; it even says it in the word," I said, attempting to joke with him a little. While I did get a tiny smile out of him, it would have been nicer to get more.

"I'm scared," he admitted. I squeezed his hand, and we fell into silence as the minutes ticked on.

CHAPTER SEVEN

AFTER MY first class the next morning, I headed back to my room. I was glad to see Rem wasn't there. I needed the privacy for a moment to be able to make a phone call I should've made a long time ago but had been scared to.

My mom picked up right away. "Hey, baby, I was getting worried. It's been two days since we talked. Last time that happened you were so sick you were nearly on your deathbed."

"Mom, I did something bad. Like really, really bad. And I just need to talk."

"Oh, Thomas, honey, you know that you could never do anything to upset us, right? We'll always love you. So, what happened? Did you cheat on a test? Plagiarize a paper? Fail a big project?"

It should have bothered me that my mom would even consider me cheating on a test to be a possibility, but I was too focused on that she said she'd always love me, and so would Dad. Even when I felt like I'd gone off the moral deep end. "No, it's nothing like that." I took a deep breath and looked across the room to Rem's bed, to where his sheets were still messed up from where we'd fallen asleep together somewhere after three that morning. "I had sex with Rem. A few times actually."

"That's great! He's so handsome. You should send us some good pictures of the two of you together for us to get framed. I knew he'd come around to seeing what a great catch you are sooner or later."

I loved my mom's optimism, and really I could have seriously used that kind of easy answer in my life. "It's not like that. He's got a girlfriend. He's had her for years, and I knew about her. I've met her and I've hung out with her and we still kept having sex. I feel horrible, and she doesn't know anything but I get around him and it's like there's nothing else in my life. It's just Rem and how much I care about him, how much I want him. Not even just sex. It's everything… he's everything."

I heard my mom sigh and prepared for the worst. But as usual she surprised me with her level of caring and understanding. "Thomas, honey, now, while I don't condone cheating, I'm never going to be one of those parents who tells their kid he's been bad for any reason. I think it's best if you try to find a way to end things with him, only because I don't think you'll be able to break them apart if you haven't already. And really, baby, if he's been around you all this time and hasn't figured out what a great person you are, I don't think he'll be able to."

I felt like crying because not only was my mom right, she was being freaking perfect right then. "That's not the worst part," I whispered as I tried to hold back my tears.

"Honey, are you in love with him? Is that what this is?"

I heard the worry in my mom's voice and knew she might have been right. Maybe I was falling in love with Rem. Maybe I was already there. But that didn't matter right now. "She's pregnant." The words hurt to say because it made them even more real than they had been the night before when it was just Angela, Rem, and I who knew. Now it was my mom, soon it would be my dad, and then it felt like everyone in Thornwood would know the guy I cared about was having a child with someone else.

My mom took a long time to say anything to me. "Do they have a plan yet?"

I shrugged. As far as I knew, they were both still in shock, unless something had changed this morning when they were in economics together. "No idea."

"Let me talk to your dad, and I'll call you back. How long do you have until your next class?"

Pulling the phone away from my ear, I checked the time. "About an hour." Unless I skipped my next class and the one that I had after it too. If I wasn't too depressed and wanting to wallow in my comfy blanket in my bed that squeaked ridiculously loudly every single time Rem and I had had sex on it. That was a very real possibility because right then I didn't want to do anything but find Rem and make him promise me this was all going to go away.

"I'll text you before your next class. Okay, sweetie? Just... I don't know. Try not to think about it. Okay?"

That was far too simple to actually work. "Sure. I'll try." I promised her that I would, but I knew it wouldn't happen that way. I would give it my best, though because she was right in that it would probably help me if I could make it here. I just didn't have all that much hope for something working out in my favor from this mess. "Talk to you later."

"Bye, Mom." I usually felt better after we hung up, but this time wasn't like the others. This time I felt just as lost and just as depressed as I had before. Only this time I was waiting for her text, but why, I had no real idea. There was nothing she had to talk to my dad about when it came to my clusterfuck of a life as far as I was concerned.

Get them together with you later today. Call me when they're there so we can all talk. I'm taking today off, her text message said.

Will do. As I headed toward my next class, I didn't even have the energy to speculate on what she wanted or why it was important enough for her to take time off from the diner, which she never did unless it was an emergency.

Once the three of us were together and we'd had dinner, I called my mom back. "Hey, they're here, and we're in the dorm room," I told her. I hadn't said anything to Rem or Angela, so it didn't really surprise me they were giving me confused looks.

"Great. First, though, I wanted to see if this idea would be okay with you, assuming that Rem and Angela agreed to it."

My mom wasn't on speakerphone, but I still glanced over to Rem to see if he'd heard. He was watching me, but he didn't seem to be acting any differently than he had before as he took Angela's hand between his own. I really needed him to hold my hand like that right about then, but of course that wasn't going to happen in this lifetime.

And I hated myself for resenting Angela just a bit for being a part of Rem's life. "What idea?" I asked my mom.

"Well… your father and I were talking, and we do have room for another child, if they were interested."

I nearly lost my balance as her idea hit me square in the chest. She wanted to…. She and Dad …. They were going to…. Oh God. I needed to sit down.

"You okay?" Rem asked me from across the room. I waved him off as I lifted myself onto the counter.

"You sure you want to do that?" I asked her.

Her soft laugh made me smile through the panic of my mom possibly raising the child of the guy I cared about. "If they chose adoption and gave this child to someone else, do you care about Rem so little that you wouldn't be wondering how the baby was doing? If they were okay? If they were safe?"

She was right, damn her. Of course she was. She knew I'd think about the child all the time, if only because they were a part of Rem. "Okay. I'll put you on speaker, and you can talk to them."

"Thank you, baby."

I hopped off the counter and went over to sit next to them on Rem's bed so they could hear my mom better. "Rem, Angela, this is Thomas's mom." There was a bit of a pause as my dad came over to the phone too. "And his dad. You can call us Mr. and Mrs. Maloney."

The formality bugged me, especially given what my mom was about to ask of them, but maybe that was my mom's point. I'd never seen them do this before, but part of me was kind of glad they were about to bring it up.

"Hi," Angela said. She sounded nervous.

Rem was still watching me, like he had no idea what I'd done. I really hoped he wasn't about to get mad at me for going to my mom for help. "Hey," he said anyway.

"You two, Thomas has told me about your coming baby, and we wanted to offer our help, if you choose adoption."

They were both staring at me now, and I shrank away a little.

"We're not…. We haven't decided anything…," Angela hedged.

"Of course not. It's all still so new and scary, I'm sure," my mom said calmly. "We've adopted before and know how overwhelming an unplanned baby can be. We just wanted to offer our help. Here's our number, and if you forget it you can always ask Thomas for it. Call us for whatever, even if you just want to talk to someone who has been pregnant before."

She rattled off her number, and I saw Angela quickly whip out her phone to take it down. "Thanks. I mean. Just…." Her voice broke a little. "Thanks."

"Anytime, sweetie. Thomas, honey, be good in your classes. Don't skip any."

My mom knew too much for her own good. "Talk to you later. Love you."

"Love you too, baby."

I hung up the phone and got up from Rem's bed to go over to my own. I expected the questions to begin, but Rem surprised me with his first one. "How old was your mom when she had you? She sounds pretty young."

It took me a moment to figure out who he was talking about. Then it hit me, and I felt stupid for not getting what he was asking right away. "My mom didn't give birth to me. She adopted me when I was an infant. My birth mom was a teenager when she got pregnant with me, and at the time my mom was on a waiting list for a baby, so I guess it just worked out." He looked at me like I was somehow weird or maybe even alien-like for being adopted. It made me feel defensive, and I frowned at him. "It's not that strange."

Rem looked away from me right away, as if he'd been able to figure out what I'd meant. Angela was still looking at me as she held her phone between her hands, though. "I can't keep this baby," she mumbled. I expected her to touch her stomach, like I'd seen some women do when talking about the babies growing inside of them, but she didn't. She just kept playing with her phone. "I can't believe we were so stupid. We've always used protection before. It's just a few times…." She shook her head, and I forced myself to look away from Rem and focus more on Angela so it wouldn't look like I was staring at him. But at the same time, I was thinking about how she was right. It was stupid of them to not use protection. Of course that made me think of my first time with Rem, though, in that laundry room and how I hadn't thought to bring any, but he did. Or were condoms always on him so he'd be ready if Angela wanted to have sex with him?

I had to stop thinking like that. And being jealous of them needed to end too. They were Rem and Angela. That's who they were and how they were going to live forever and ever. There was no me and Rem and her and him too. There just couldn't be. Life didn't work that way.

Rem laid his forehead against Angela's shoulder. I recognized it as the same thing he did with me when he was upset or worried. I desperately wanted to reach over to him, to touch him, to make everything better for him. "I don't want you to have an abortion. I know it's not really my call and it's your body, but it's my baby too. And I don't want you to have an abortion. Please." He was begging her, his voice unusually soft, and I wanted to add my voice as well, even though my opinion didn't matter. But I chose to stay quiet and out of their conversation. I really shouldn't even have still been there.

Angela reached up and ran her fingers through his curls. I knew how soft they were, especially when he went without gel or mousse. His curls were natural today, just the way I liked them. She'd convinced him to shave, but I got him to go without putting stuff in his hair. "I don't want an abortion either. But I can't keep this baby."

The relief on Rem's face was obvious. "I can't either. We're too young."

Angela nodded. "My parents would kill us. Literally."

Rem smiled, just a little bit, but it was there. "Yeah. The senator would come after me with his shotgun." I hadn't known Angela's dad was a senator, but then again I didn't know much about her at all. I realized in that moment, everything I knew about her was from Rem, and I only thought about her in relation to him and not as her own person. That wasn't fair to her, and I vowed to get to know her better, especially if my parents were really considering adopting their baby.

"Thomas?" she asked me.

I refocused on her. "Yes?"

"Are your parents good? I mean, did you like them... er...." She blushed deeply and hid her face in Rem's shirt. "Sorry."

I chuckled. "It's fine. I'm glad they adopted me. I mean, I couldn't have asked for a better reaction when I came out to them."

Her eyes got really wide, and I realized Rem hadn't told her I was gay. I'd also never mentioned it to her. I glanced at Rem, who was purposefully looking anywhere but me. "I didn't know that you were gay. Rem, did you?"

Rem shook his head. "Nope. Not that I care, but I had no idea." He lied so fucking well. I tried not to glare at him, but I'm sure I did a little bit. At least Angela didn't seem to notice me doing it. Small miracles.

"I don't either." She gave me a little smile. Maybe it was supposed to be reassuring or something like that. Really, though, I was too busy thinking about other stuff. Like how in the hell I was supposed to be okay with her being pregnant with his child. Okay, well that was more than a little bit selfish, I realized. But the feeling remained harbored within me.

Angela hung out with us for another few hours before she had to go back to her dorm room because of curfew. She hugged Rem as she left, then hugged me too. "You're such a great friend," she told me.

I nodded. "You are too." Damn, it hurt how easy it was to lie to her. I closed the door behind her, then waited for her footsteps to go down the hall before I came away from the door.

"There's probably still some places open if you wanted to go out for pizza or something. Or a movie," Rem offered.

I shook my head. I wasn't really in the mood anymore. I sat down next to him on his bed, right where Angela had been, and I sighed loudly. It didn't make me feel any better. "I'm going to move into another room at the end of the semester. For real this time."

"Don't. I need you here with me."

Rolling my eyes, I wished that wasn't true. And I wished I didn't want him next to me all the time. Or that I didn't need him just as much as he seemed to need me. "I don't know if I can do this anymore, though," I whispered to him. "I want to be your friend, and I want all of you, all the time, but Angela is pregnant now. I don't want to be your way of cheating on your pregnant girlfriend."

He slid his hand into mine, and I looked down at our joined hands on the blanket. We fit together so well, no matter how we were. But it seemed life had other ideas. "Be my friend, then," he said.

I nodded. I could try my best to be his friend. "Nothing more than that. Nothing at all."

Rem laid his head on my shoulder, and I turned my face so I could kiss him on his forehead, just one more time. For the last time, I knew. Holding hands was fine. I'd hold him too, if he needed me. But my lips would never touch his again. I'd make sure of it. No more kisses, no more anything. Never getting to be with him again nearly broke my heart, but then I thought about Angela and how much she'd need him in the coming months. And I started to get over myself a little.

"You promise me that there won't be anything else, and I'll stay."

He nodded, and even though he was good at lying, I chose to believe him. I needed to. "Best friends. Nothing more."

I could be best friends with a guy I cared so much about, I decided. We needed each other, and so I'd stay. "Okay. Roommates and best friends."

"Thanks for staying."

I leaned my head back against the wall and closed my eyes. Damn this day. "Sure. No problem." Don't ruin this, I told myself. Don't fall for him. Too late, but that was my problem, and Rem had enough to deal with, without me adding to his mess. I was infinitely glad I was gay since I'd never have to deal with a pregnant girlfriend. I liked kids, but I did not envy Rem's current position in life.

"Adoption is best, right?"

"I can't make that decision for you. It's up to you and Angela."
I was alive because my biological mom had chosen adoption. I
didn't blame people who chose abortion. I knew that I couldn't make
decisions for other people, and that was a really big one to make. But
I was glad that Angela wasn't going to have an abortion. I couldn't do
anything about it if she changed her mind, but for Rem I hoped she
didn't. And I really wanted to have my parents take care of their baby,
because my mom was right—I would have worried about it. Rem and
I may never speak again after college, but his kid would still be safe
and taken care of because of my parents.

"Do you ever think about your birth mom?" he asked me.

I shrugged. "Sometimes. I used to think about her a lot more
when I was younger. I always knew that I was adopted, but I never
tried to go find her or anything like that. She did the best thing she
could for me, and that was giving me up."

"Even if we don't take your mom up on her offer and find an
adoption agency instead, I do appreciate her offer."

"Why wouldn't you?" Maybe I snapped a little because he
seemed to move away and off my shoulder like I'd bothered him with
my question. But I hadn't meant to ask him so bluntly.

He shrugged, though. "Maybe I don't want to wonder how the
baby is all the time. Maybe I can't handle it. Maybe Angela won't
want all of our lives tied together forever if she ever finds out about
us. There's a lot of maybes here."

"Okay. I understand that." I didn't think there was any reason
she would ever find out about what we'd been doing, but then again,
perhaps he'd come clean someday and tell her about everyone. If all
of his cheating ever came out, I knew how hurt she'd probably be
because I could see how much she loved him. It was obvious just
looking at them. I'd have been hurt too if I'd been in her place. I'd
never been cheated on that I knew of, but it had to suck in the worst
kind of way.

He sighed and took his head off my shoulder. "Tell me about
Thornwood, about your family."

Frowning, I turned to look at him as he leaned back against the wall next to me. "Why?"

Rem smiled weakly without looking over at me. "Because I want to think about the little kid, my kid, having a life there. Please?"

"Sure. I guess. Well, Thornwood is tiny. I can walk from one end to the other in about twenty minutes. We've got a few cops that work out of a business office. My mom works at the diner and has for decades. It's really the only place to eat in town unless you want to get something from the deli at the grocery store. My first job was at that diner. I bussed tables."

Rem's smile grew. "Do they have good pie?"

"Yeah, the best. My parents live in a townhouse. It's not big, but it's never felt all that tight to me. I've always had to share a room because my parents have always fostered kids. The grocery store is right behind the townhouse, which is on a row of townhouses that all look the same. There's really only one road through Thornwood, and we're in the mountains, so there's plenty of trees around and loads of deer and foxes all the time."

Rem pulled his fingers back so he was rubbing them against my palm, tickling me, instead of just holding my hand. I pulled my feet up and rested my knees against my chest. "It sounds nice. I can almost picture them. A little boy with my hair running through the woods. You'd take care of him? And watch over him?"

I nodded, knowing I'd keep that promise to him. He didn't even have to ask me that. "I'll catch frogs with him and teach him how to put up a tent. And we can paint with finger paints in the park in the summer and make snowmen in the winter."

Rem leaned over and pressed his lips to my shoulder. I wish we could have done more without me hating myself afterward for it. "I want that kind of life for him. It's everything Angela and I can't give him. I need to focus on football, and Angela...." Rem shook his head. "She can't be a mom right now. We aren't old enough, aren't ready. We don't want it enough. I know that. There are plenty of people who have babies when they are younger than we are and make it work. But I know we can't have the kinds of lives that we want and still be parents to that baby. Is that selfish? Am I a horrible person for thinking that?"

I quickly shook my head. "I don't think you are."

"Thanks. Lie down with me for a while? Please?"

I pursed my lips. "Rem... I don't want to have sex with you." That was a lie. "I can't. Not now that she's pregnant. We just went over this." It made me a little frustrated that he'd even ask me that right now, since we'd really just talked about not being anything more than friends.

He smirked at me. "I'm asking you to lie next to me. To hold me and I hold you, and we pretend that my girlfriend isn't pregnant for a little while."

Pretending wouldn't change anything, I knew. But it felt good to stretch out on the bed next to him and have him pressed up against me. I put my arm over his stomach and rested my forehead in his curls. He rested his hand over mine, and sometime later that night, I fell asleep with him still in my arms.

CHAPTER EIGHT

ANGELA STARTED showing right around the second week of November, and her friends said it was cute she was wearing more and more of Rem's shirts. They didn't know what she was hiding, and as we sat there together watching Rem be the Crusader's quarterback in his shiny purple uniform, it was kind of nice to be in on the secret. She took my hand, as she had started doing more and more, and we sat together watching the man we both loved get sacked repeatedly. Watching him was fun; watching him getting beaten up, though, was pretty much torture. We groaned and cringed together and laughed when we saw him get back up smiling.

"You're the best kind of guy friend. I feel completely safe with you," she said to me while we waited for Rem to get cleaned up.

I gave her a smile and bumped my shoulder against hers. I pretended being in love with Rem, since I was sure I was, didn't make me a bad person. We'd stopped having sex. What we'd done before, that was okay. It wasn't great, but then this dancing around each other and pretending we didn't want each other wasn't ideal either. I told myself it was better than nothing, though, and some days I even started to believe it.

As the weeks hurried along into winter, I found myself thinking more and more about those first few days when we'd moved in together, back when I hadn't known Angela existed, back when it was just me and Rem and we'd had sex and touched each other as often as we wanted to. I missed those times more than I would ever admit.

Angela ate dinner with us most nights, and her birthday was no different. We ordered Chinese, and I was glad when my fortune cookie didn't say anything about me coming clean to my friend to make me feel even worse. While they cuddled on Rem's bed, I threw out the trash. He rubbed her stomach, but she didn't ever touch the baby that I could tell.

"Did your parents wonder why you didn't go home for your birthday?" I asked her.

She shook her head. "Not really. I told them Rem and I were going away for the weekend a few weeks back, just to cover our bases. They think we're in Cancun. We went there in high school and loved it, so it wasn't that much of a stretch for them, I guess."

"Must have been nice." Rem looked over at me, and I hoped I didn't let too much jealousy come into my words.

Angela just smiled at me. "It was. You should come with us sometime. You know, after all this is over."

"All this" being the baby I guessed. Right…. "Sure. Sounds good." I knew I wouldn't be going anywhere with the two of them. Rem, yes, I'd go around the world with him if he asked me to. But with Angela over every day, it was hard to pretend I didn't want Rem when she was around. At night when she had to go back to her own dorm was the only time I could be absolutely sure I'd have Rem to myself, and I never wasted any of that time.

As soon as she left for the night, Rem was in my bed, and I held him. This had almost become a nightly routine for us. She would go, and then he would be mine. "I don't think you should go to Cancun with us," he said as he tangled his fingers up in mine.

We'd stripped down to just our underwear, something I'd started wearing more and more as we'd taken to lying together at night, and I liked the feeling of his bare legs against mine. "Don't worry, there's no way in hell I'm taking a vacation with you two."

Rem froze in my arms, and I realized that probably came out a little more harshly than I'd meant them to. "You hate her that much?"

I shook my head. "I don't hate her at all. I like her. She's really nice. But I want you too much." *I love you too much.* I wanted to say the words, but they wouldn't have made a difference now, and he didn't need to hear them. They wouldn't have changed anything between us. I was sure of it.

TWO WEEKS before fall break, Rem and Angela sat me down after we'd finished pizza for dinner. Rem looked resigned while Angela appeared to almost be relieved. "Thomas, we've decided to let your parents adopt the baby," she said. I noticed how she didn't say "our" baby.

"Okay. I'll call them." I took out my phone to do just that and put them on speakerphone when the line connected. "Hey."

"Thomas! I made green goo! And now my hands are green!"

I caught Rem's smile. "That's great, buddy. Can you get my mom on the phone please? Or my dad? Doesn't matter."

"Mrs. Maloney!"

I cringed at his screeching yell.

"Dusty! Child, what are you doing? Go get washed up! This green had better be food coloring!" I heard him laughing as he ran up what sounded like the stairs, which ran through the middle of the townhouse. "I swear, some days that child…. Hello?"

I was smiling. "Hey, Mom."

"Oh, good, one child of mine that doesn't drive me crazy. When you're home for winter break you're going to help me repaint these cabinets. Dusty decorated them with green handprints. You've been warned."

Laughing, I shook my head. "Sure. Whatever you need. Mom, I'm calling because Rem and Angela have made a decision regarding their baby." I'd call it theirs, even if Angela wouldn't.

She got quiet for a moment. "Oh?" I knew she might be worried if they hadn't decided on her, maybe even a little disappointed. My mom loved babies, after all. And I would have also been worried about the baby growing up somewhere else.

Angela leaned forward a little. "We'd like you to adopt it. So, how do we do it? Do we sign some papers or something?"

"Are you sure?" my mom asked her.

Rem didn't look so sure, but Angela nodded. "Yes. If I could give it to you right now, I would. I don't want it. What do we need to do?"

"Okay. Thank you, Angela. And you too, Rem. Give Thomas your e-mail addresses, and I'll send you pictures of our house, all of our adoption stuff, and background checks from the agency we work with so that you'll know everything about us. And we'll have our lawyer draw up an adoption agreement. We can go over it as many times as you need to so that you both feel comfortable relinquishing your baby to us. Would you like to meet us? You could both fly back here with Thomas for winter break and spend a week with us. We'd love to have you here in Thornwood."

I loved that idea and couldn't wait to show Rem around my hometown. "I'd like that," he said.

Angela didn't look so sure. "I don't need to." Rem shot her a look. "But it will be nice. Sure. We'll come visit you."

My mom sounded so much happier. I could practically see her smiling now. And she'd get to meet Rem, which was important to me because she knew how much I cared about him. "Perfect. I look forward to meeting you both. In the meantime, Angela, I'll set up an account with the school's health care clinic for all of your prenatal stuff. They'll have a credit card on file for all of your appointments. If you already have a team with you, please let me know, but if you don't, this will be completely private, and your parents will never know about the baby if you're worried about that."

Angela smiled, and it looked completely relaxed, much more so than I'd seen from her recently. "Thanks. I haven't been to the doctor yet. I know I need to."

"And right away too," my mom agreed with her. "We need to make sure everything is okay with your little one. If you don't want to find out the baby's sex, you don't have to. We don't mind a surprise. But if anything comes up in any scans, please let us know. We won't change our minds about adopting, but we want to make sure we have doctors in place if the baby needs specialized care in any way. Dear, when are you due?"

Angela chewed on her bottom lip a little. "June. I think. I'll know more after I go to the doctor, I guess. I'm just glad I'll be able to finish the semester without having to worry about giving birth in the middle of finals." She laughed a little, and I wished she would have cared more about her baby. But maybe she just didn't want to.

"Well that is good, then. I'll set up everything with the clinic tomorrow morning when they open. Thank you both for thinking of us. We'll send you three tickets to come here on your break too. We're looking forward to meeting you two. Thomas, honey, I need to go make dinner, so we'll talk later, okay?"

"Yep. Bye. Love you."

She blew me a kiss through the phone. "Love you too, baby." She hung up, and I looked at the two of them.

"Are your parents rich?" Angela asked me.

I shook my head. "Nope. Not at all. They have their priorities, though."

When we were alone again I couldn't wait to get my arms around Rem. It was getting harder and harder not to touch him, not to want him all the damn time. I pressed my face into his curls.

"I missed you today," he said as the TV made noise in the background. It might have been an action movie. Or something to do with a zombie. I wasn't really sure, and I didn't really care, either.

"I was right here with you the whole time."

He rubbed his hands over my arms, and I felt him laugh before I actually heard it. "Yeah. But I couldn't touch you. I couldn't hold you." He turned over in my arms, and suddenly I was looking down at him as he moved so he was holding me too. "And I couldn't kiss you today while she was here."

I pursed my lips and began to pull away, but he shook his head. "I want you, but I know we can't," he said.

Fine. I relaxed against him. And yes, it was nice to hold him and to be held. God I missed this so fucking much. I missed his little bit of stubble, and feeling his curls under my fingertips, and as I snuck a kiss against his throat, I realized how much I missed that too.

"I want you too," I told him softly, in case he couldn't already tell that for himself. I even pushed my hips a little into his, but then I froze above him when he dug his fingers into my back and opened his mouth a little on a gasp. "Sorry." I was blushing, and I wanted to get off him, but at the same time I wanted to stay right where I was. I groaned as I lay down on top of him and tried not to feel him moving under me.

"It's okay," he mumbled. He sighed and relaxed his fingers on my back. "I wish we could."

I nodded. I did too. I laid my forehead against his and closed my eyes. The minutes ticked by. The TV played on, but it all faded into the background as we lay together and I focused only on him.

"You'll take care of the child right?" he whispered a few minutes later. I pulled away a little so that I could see his face, and he shifted his gaze to mine. His beautiful green eyes were wet, and I kissed his cheek. I wanted to kiss his lips, to try to take away his worries and his pain and lose myself with him for a while, but we couldn't.

So I did the only thing I could do. I made him a promise. "Always. You won't have to worry about them. I promise."

Rem gave me a weak smile and blinked away some of his tears. He didn't move to brush them off his cheeks, but I leaned forward to kiss them away. "I'll feel better knowing they're with you."

"My parents will take care of them too. They love kids." It wouldn't just be me. In fact it wouldn't be me most of the time, but I knew I belonged in Colorado, and with Rem's child going there, I was sure I wouldn't be straying too far from the place I'd always known as my home. Miami was nice, and I liked the ocean well enough, but I missed the mountains, the pine trees, the deer and the elk, and sometimes I even missed the lack of humidity. It kept my hair from frizzing up like Rem's did sometimes.

"Would they have done this for us if we didn't care about each other?"

I didn't ask him how he knew I'd talked to my parents about us, but he didn't seem like he cared. I shrugged. I didn't have a certain answer for him. "Maybe. They've always rushed in to help any child in need. But if they didn't know how much I care about you, maybe they would have just referred you to the agency they work with and said they'd help in whatever way they could rather than adopting your baby themselves."

Rem shook his head. "Not mine."

I moved my hands around his cheeks so I could frame his face and make him look at me. "Yes, the baby is. With adoption you'll give up your rights to the baby, but it won't stop being yours to you. I think you'll always care about that baby."

"But what will it matter?" he asked me softly. "If the baby isn't mine, if he never knows me, then what does it matter if I love him? If I never stop thinking about him? If I hold Angela more now than I have in the last two years only to get close to my child?" He gave me a push, and I rolled off him as he sat up at the edge of my bed.

His shoulders shook, and I wrapped my arms around him from behind. I knelt with a knee on either side of his hips, and he lifted his hands to cover my hands with his on his chest. "It'll be okay," I whispered to him.

"I wish I was older and in a better place to have a child. And I wish I could have that child and have you too," he told me.

I nodded. "I want that too." He fell into silence and cried, and I just tried not to cry right along with him.

CHAPTER NINE

THE NEXT morning, I followed Angela as she and Rem held hands on their way to the nearest OBGYN clinic, which was pretty close to campus. The sun was shining. People smiled around me and some even waved to me. And I just tried to be happy for Rem and Angela. When she smiled at me, I smiled back. When Rem looked at me I tried to act like a friend and not like someone who wanted him more than anything.

She'd been able to snag the first appointment of the day because someone had cancelled at the last minute. I sat in the waiting room on an awful little plastic chair, while she and Rem went in for her first prenatal exam. It was stupid to be jealous of her or to want Rem all to myself. I knew even if she wasn't in his life he still couldn't have been mine. He was trying too hard to be straight, and I couldn't be a secret forever.

The appointment took nearly an hour, and when they were done, Angela was on the phone and talking in quiet whispers. "What's going on?" I asked Rem as I got up to greet them.

He gave me a little smile and bumped my shoulder with his while Angela was looking away from us. "She's talking to your parents. The baby's fine." The relief in his voice was obvious, and I gave him a big smile.

"That's great."

He nodded. "Yeah. It is." I wanted to hug him, to kiss him, to hold his hand. Fuck. I just wanted to touch him, and the need was so great that I had to step back to put some space between us before I gave in and took what I knew I couldn't have.

Angela hugged me as soon as she was off the phone, and I wondered why it was okay to hug her and not Rem. Why could she kiss my cheek and hold my hand and hug me whenever she wanted to but I could do none of that to Rem? Oh yeah, that's right. Because I fucking wanted him every minute of every damn day, and Angela was just a friend, and I was her gay friend that let her hang out in our dorm room all the time.

Rem gave me a sympathetic look as if he knew even one ounce of what I was thinking. I really doubted he did, and maybe I'd misinterpreted his look completely. "Your mom's excited," Angela told me.

I nodded and let her out of my arms when she pulled back. I didn't dislike her, but I always waited for her to break our hugs first so she didn't think that I was eager to get away from her. It was one of the many things I figured I probably did to cover up how much I cared about Rem.

"I'm happy for you both." I said the words to her, but I was looking at Rem. He gave me a nod, barely more than the tilt of his chin, but I saw it. "Time to get to class?"

"Yeah. Spanish." Rem made a face, and I laughed.

"Don't act like it's a hard class for you," I told him as we headed out of the building.

He shook his head, and when Angela reached for his hand again, he took it. It was so easy for them to hold hands. It wasn't like the campus was homophobic or anything like that, so if Rem was out, I could have held his hand too. Only he wasn't, and wouldn't be, and I needed to get over the idea that I'd ever be able to walk around in daylight with his hand in mine.

"I have composition," Angela said with a sigh. "I hate that class."

Snickering, I shook my head. "I do too." I'd wanted to test out of it, but they wouldn't let me. "I'm going to biology."

Angela kissed me on my cheek when we parted ways. Her class was to the south of campus and Rem and I were in the west. "Muggy today," Rem told me as he fanned his shirt a little over his stomach, exposing abs—perfect for licking—built from hours of practicing football.

"It's always muggy here," I grumbled as I forced my mind away from his stomach. We shared a smile.

With our hands swinging between us while we walked, sometimes my fingers brushed against his. I tried not to focus on that brief contact. "In less than a month, we'll be with your parents. I've never met parents before."

I knew what he was saying. He'd never met the parents of a guy he'd had sex with before. "They'll like you. And they know not to say anything." About us, I didn't add. We were careful about what we said in public, even when there weren't that many people around. His cover was important to him, and I wasn't going to be the one to out him.

He nodded, and we went to our classes. That afternoon Angela stopped by my dorm, and we walked together to go see Rem play football. Every time I watched him in his damn purple jersey I thought about the first night I had with him. When I saw him sitting there in the kitchen with a little smile on his face and a purple mask over his cheeks. Where he pushed me up against a dryer and gave me everything I wanted from him.

While Angela sat beside me and had her hand in mine, I felt sick thinking about him being inside of me, him digging his fingers into my shoulder as he came with his cock deep within me.

People wore sweaters around me, and I focused on how weird it was for people to act like it was cold in Miami as they sat there bundled up in their scarves and gloves. I wore shorts and flip-flops. Always. An inch of snow back home, and I was still in flip-flops. I might have put on a hoodie, but I wasn't getting on boots for anything less than four inches, and maybe not even then.

Thinking about home and Thanksgiving coming up was a nice distraction, and it helped me get through the game and even clap and cheer when I was supposed to. We laughed together as we walked back to the dorms, and I leaned against the wall when they kissed good night.

As soon as we were alone together, Rem stripped off his clothes, leaving just his boxers, and wrapped himself around me as we lay in bed together. We were in his, but it didn't matter. They were both the same, and we brought our pillows and blankets with us to whichever one we went to. He put on a movie, drank a protein shake, and we spent the rest of the night together with my fingers tangled in his curls and his arms around my shoulders.

Thanksgiving had never been a holiday where my family stood around cooking this huge meal and tons of people came over to say what they were thankful for like in the movies. I didn't even know what that would have been like. Maybe we went easy on the day since my mom was always working with food anyway, and no one thought she should have still been doing it then. Sometimes Mom worked on the holidays, though. The diner was open twenty-four hours a day, seven days a week, though it was hardly ever busy enough to be. But it was one of the few places to get real food if you were going through the mountains and weren't planning to stop at the casinos for their buffet.

So when we ordered Chinese food for Thanksgiving and the three of us ate while sitting on the floor and laughing over an old movie, it felt pretty perfect to me. Angela sat between Rem's thighs, and he fed her while keeping a hand on her stomach, right over his child. I wondered if she could tell, like I could, how much more affectionate he'd become since she became pregnant. I wondered what she thought about it, if she realized he loved his child but only thought of her as a good friend whom he didn't want to hurt.

It didn't really matter, I knew, but I still thought about it as we sat there together with our secrets hanging out there in the room with us. They never felt more suffocating than when the three of us were together in our dorm room. He kissed her, and they cuddled on the bed I'd shared with him the night before when they were done eating on the floor. It hurt to see, but it sucked to think about.

When they fell asleep together in a post-gorge nap, I went for a walk. The campus was practically deserted, and I found myself by the water again. I closed my eyes, and the feeling of the wind and the surf's spray against my face helped calm me as I went to the lonely little outcropping.

I felt like I had my head on straight, and so I called my mom. "Hey. Happy Thanksgiving," I told her.

"Happy Thanksgiving. What are you up to? What did you get to eat?"

I found a smooth place on the rocks and sat down to watch the waves. "I'm at the beach right now, and we just finished our Chinese food. Angela ate with us. She's starting to show a lot more now. She's so skinny, so any extra weight around her stomach is pretty noticeable, even though she's still really early in her pregnancy. And Rem…." My voice cracked, and I shut my mouth as quickly as I could.

"Oh, my baby, I hope he knows how much you love him."

I shook my head and wiped at my eyes as tears that had no right to come out began streaming down my cheeks. "He doesn't. We don't talk about that. It hurts too much." I was shaking now as I wrapped my arms around myself and tried not to cry any more than I already had. "I gotta go."

"Thomas…."

I couldn't talk to her and cry at the same time, and my tears seemed to be winning out. "Mom. I gotta go."

She sighed. "Okay. We'll talk when you're here, though. Your dad and I were thinking that we don't think it's a good idea for you to go back after this semester. Not if being around him breaks your heart so much. You don't say anything, but I can tell when my son is hurting."

"I don't want to be here either," I whispered through my tears. It felt like giving up, like running away, like being a coward all because I couldn't handle living with the man I loved and watching him be with someone else. I was better than that, but Rem and I, and how much I cared about him… that was bigger than me, and I was so tired of fighting it all the time.

"We'll take care of everything. If you decide to stay, if you change your mind, that's okay too. I just want you to be happy. You're my baby."

I sniffled and wiped at my eyes. "Yeah, I know. Bye, Mom."

"Bye, Baby Boy."

The old nickname was good to hear. When she'd adopted me, I hadn't had a name. Not a real one anyway. And so they'd called me Baby Boy for the first few months. I don't remember any of that of course, but they had plenty of videos of me from that time and, as strange as it is, to me Baby Boy was my first name.

I sat there on the rocks for a long time, well past when the sun started to go down, and when I heard pebbles moving behind me, I thought it was one of the beach patrollers coming over to check on me and make sure I was still alive or something. But it was Rem who sat down next to me on the narrow little rock outcropping.

"Hey," he said.

I hoped he thought my face was red from the wind and not because I'd spent the past few hours crying. "Hi," I choked out. Maybe he'd be convinced I was hoarse from the wind too.

Rem was close enough that our thighs could have touched, that we could have kissed. If we could have. It wasn't a matter of wanting, I knew. It was a matter of being able to, of his choices and what he wanted getting in the way of us. My hands lay in my lap, and he took one of them. We were far enough away from everything that people couldn't see us, I didn't think, and I loved that he was willing to be even a little affectionate with me outside of our room.

"I won't be coming back after this semester," I told him.

He didn't say anything to me at first, just rubbed his free hand over mine. "I'm probably going to ask Angela to marry me soon, so we'd be moving to an apartment off campus anyway."

I tried to pull my hand away, but he held onto me too tightly. "You don't even love her," I hissed at him.

He nodded and briefly touched his forehead against my shoulder. "When we were talking about the baby, about how we could give it up for adoption, about how she didn't have to have an abortion…." He licked his lips and looked up at me for only a second before looking away from me again. "She talked about how much she loved me and how giving up this one baby would be okay because we'd have more of them once we were married and had a house and I had a pro football career. I can't hurt her anymore."

"You should get married. You should go have your perfect life together," I snapped at him sarcastically. This time when I yanked my hand out of his, he let me go. But I didn't get up. I wasn't ready to walk away from him yet. Damn it, I still wanted to be right there with him. Because being close to Rem, just being able to share his space was better than nothing, and right then in that moment, I needed him so fucking much.

"I want you at the wedding. Please."

I was quick to shake my head. There was no way in hell I was going to go to that thing, and he was an ass for saying he wanted me there with him. "No. You want the guy you cheated on your girlfriend with to be at your wedding?"

"I want my best friend there with me," he countered.

"I can't, Rem. I won't. I care about you too much to be there pretending to be happy for you as I watch you marry someone else. It hurts too much just to see you two together now." I started crying again, and Rem put his arm around my shoulders and cried right along with me.

SINCE I knew I'd be leaving Miami College at the end of the semester, winter break couldn't come soon enough. I missed home, I missed my family, and I even missed Dusty and his nearly constant messes. But as the weeks blew past me, I realized my time with Rem was coming to a close. I loved him, but neither of us said that, not since the night on the beach when I'd confessed my feelings to him and he'd said nothing back to me. I knew he cared about me. I could tell it every time he touched my hands or gave me a hug. Or when we lay together at night. But it wasn't the same as hearing the words. And I was sure I'd never hear them from him.

We flew to Colorado together, and I had everything I'd come to Miami with, plus a few sweatshirts for my parents. Angela didn't know I wasn't coming back yet, but unless she missed the giant amount of stuff I'd pushed into the taxi, she had to have some idea. She didn't say anything, though.

Dusty was the first one to see me at Denver International. He ran up to me, and I nearly cried as I hugged him. Damn it was good to have my family back with me.

"Dusty, this is Rem and Angela," I quickly introduced them all. Then I saw my mom, and even though he clung to me as tightly as he could, I put Dusty down so I could hug her.

"My baby boy," she said, kissing my cheeks and smoothing back my hair. It'd become a huge mess when I'd fallen asleep on a layover in Chicago. "And you two of course need no introduction to me. Rem, Angela, welcome to Colorado."

She let me go to hug them, and Dusty forced himself back into my arms. Damn kid. Dad gave me a handshake in his stoic way, but he smiled at me and gave me a wink after looking Rem over. That made me blush.

It took about two hours to get home, but by then we were all starving, and thank God it was Saturday because mom got right to work on her pancakes. Suddenly it was okay that we'd taken the red-eye as I sat there stuffing my face with one that was the shape of a wave. Dusty got a cowboy hat, Dad had a hammer, Angela had a purse, and Rem, fuck he looked good sitting in the kitchen I'd grown up in surrounded by my family. Rem was eating a football-shaped pancake.

"These are really good," he told my mom. And that was the end of it. She loved him too.

A week with him went by too fast, probably because it was my last week with him ever and because we never got any time alone. I showed him the woods that went around Thornwood, the diner where my mom worked, the grocery store that was hard to miss because it was basically the view from anywhere in the back of the house, and the school I'd gone to. The school wasn't technically in Thornwood, but it was the only one in the area, and it supported all twelve grades, so his child would be going there too.

We went for a walk together while Angela was resting on the last day they'd be there. I'd been pulling away, not wanting to spend too much time with Rem since this would be the last I'd have with him, and it hurt too much. But now that I wouldn't ever have him close to me again, I wished I'd never left his side in all the months I'd known him.

We went into the woods, and once we were beyond the tree line, he took my hand. It felt so good to be touched by him, to be wanted. Just to be near to him enough that there didn't seem to be any space between us.

"I'm going to miss you," he said as we kept walking away from town.

I nodded. "I'll miss you too."

We found a big tree, and he leaned me back against it. I should have told him not to kiss me or pushed him away or something, but I didn't. We kissed, and I cried because it was the last kiss we'd ever have.

He lifted up my shirt and rested his hands against my stomach. December in Colorado wasn't exactly warm, but I didn't mind the chill as long as he just kept touching me. "You'll take care of my child?" he made me promise again.

"Yes. Always." Another kiss and I tasted the chocolate cake my mom had made on his tongue. I dug my fingers into the back of his shirt, right above the waist of his pants, and I never wanted to let him go. He was mine, but only in that moment.

We'd always have those stolen moments between us to remember, at least I knew that I would, but that didn't matter when all I wanted was him. I was eighteen and in love for the first time in my life. Only it was with someone I couldn't have, and it broke my heart to remember that every fucking minute of every damn day.

"Please," he whispered against my lips.

I nodded and turned around to face the tree. Whatever he wanted I would have given him. And sex in the woods about a mile from my house was completely within reason. Especially when it was our last time together. He didn't have any condoms on him, but that didn't matter to me. Lube was also nonexistent, but whatever. We got by. And when the pain lessened and all I knew was that I was with Rem again, that was all that mattered. He came in me, I came on the leaves by our feet, and we stayed like that for a long time with me pressed against the rough bark of the tree and the snow falling around us. Tears fell down my cheeks, and when we did pull apart and I turned around to face him again, I saw that he was crying too.

"Thank you."

I waited for his smile, the one he gave me after the first time we'd had sex at that stupid party, but it didn't come. I nodded and wiped roughly at my eyes. Going back home after that was hard, because it meant Rem would be leaving soon.

I went to the airport with them to say good-bye, and I hugged Angela. She'd found out I wasn't coming back, and she was mad at me about it, but she still kissed my cheek. I had to say good-bye to Rem next, but holding out my hand and waiting for him to shake it felt so shallow. I hugged him, even if he didn't want to hug me, even if Angela was watching. I hugged him, and I kept hugging him, and fuck everyone else because I loved him, and I didn't ever want to let him go. But I had to, and when he stepped back after giving me an awkward pat on my back, I released him. Because I had to, and there was nothing else to do.

"Rem, Angela, I'll see you both in June," my mom said to them. They hugged her too. "Call me whenever. I'll always answer."

They promised to call her often. No one promised to call me, and I stared at Rem's back as he walked away and took Angela's hand in his.

"Thomas, honey, let's go home," Mom said. I nodded. I was ready to go. But I waited until Rem and Angela got on the escalator to go down to the security area and I couldn't see them anymore, before I turned away. Rem might have looked back at me. I hoped he did. But maybe he'd been too focused on his girlfriend to notice me watching the man I loved as he walked out of my life.

"Do you want to know what the adoption plan might be?" Dad asked me as we piled back into the SUV to go home.

I shrugged. "Sure." Dusty and the baby were thankfully with a sitter, someone from the diner, which meant I got to spread out and take up all of the backseat with my misery.

Mom handed me the plan, and I read it over. Rem and Angela intended to give up their rights, but they were still welcome to call each year on the child's birthday to check up on them if they wanted to. Pictures and videos could be sent that day too. And it was a semiopen adoption, so the baby would know about themselves and where they came from.

"It isn't a good-bye forever," Mom tried to reassure me when I handed the plan back to her. It was different than what I had expected Rem and Angela to want, but I saw my mom's handwriting next to the mentions of once a year phone calls and pictures and I figured that, for whatever reason, Rem and Angela hadn't wanted to have much contact with their child after it was born. Or maybe just Angela hadn't. I knew Rem was hurting right now. "Thank you," I whispered to her through my tears that had started to fall.

She nodded and kissed her fingertips before putting them against my cheek. "It'll be okay. I know first loves are hard to get over. But things will be better eventually."

I knew she was right. She had to be. But right then it hurt too much for me to believe her. Everything hurt too much.

CHAPTER TEN

MADELINE ANDREA Maloney was born on June seventh at ten fifteen in the morning. Mom and Dad were there, but I'd chosen not to go. I hadn't been busy; I just hadn't wanted to sit there and see Rem and Angela together again. I didn't want to see him cry. Mom sent me pictures, though, and videos, and I held on to them, staring at my phone as I saw Rem hold his daughter for the first and last time. I saw the happiness and the heartbreak there in his beautiful green eyes, and I sat on my bed and cried for him.

Mom and Dad stayed in Miami for over a month after Madeline was born in order to finalize the adoption, but when they got back, I was on baby patrol. The thing was, I didn't mind it so much. Dusty I would have avoided as a baby, but I was the first one to go to Madeline in the mornings, and I fed her a bottle in the middle of the night when she woke up. It was hard to look at her for the first few months because I kept seeing Rem, and everything about her reminded me of him, but damn she was cute, and then it became nearly impossible for me not to be around her. She was all I had of Rem. Even though she wasn't my daughter and my parents took care of her most of the time, she spent a lot of time with me. Her first year went by so fast between me going to school online and taking care of her that when Mom answered the phone and said in a really loud voice "Hello, Angela, how are you sweetheart?" I could hardly believe it. They talked for a good hour or so, not even all about Madeline. And I waited for my phone to ring too.

Three hours later when Rem still hadn't called, I lifted Madeline off my chest and carried her into the kitchen where Mom was making the pies for the diner. "If Rem had called, you'd tell me right?" I asked her.

"Of course I would. He hasn't."

I nodded and headed back to the living room. Rem didn't call by dinner or by the time my shows were on TV and Dusty and I sat down with Madeline to watch them. I started thinking maybe he'd forgotten, but as I was saying good night to Madeline, my phone started vibrating in my pocket.

"Hello?" I whispered so that I didn't wake her.

"Hey."

I smiled and slowly backed away from her crib. "Hi. You got a new number." God he sounded good.

"Yeah. So. It's been a year."

I nodded and went into my room, which I shared with Dusty, but he was downstairs begging for another cookie before bed, so I knew I'd be alone with Rem for a while. "It has. Do you want to know about her?"

"What can you tell me?"

Mom and Dad hadn't put any kind of restrictions on the information I could pass on to him so I shrugged. "Anything you want."

"Is she walking yet?" he asked me.

I laughed. "Yeah. She is. Only a little bit right now, but she likes to try to chase me when we're playing in the living room. She talks too. Small words, of course, but she does talk."

"What was her first word?"

I missed talking to him, missed hearing his voice, missed having him next to me. "Tree. We were out together, and I was holding her a few months ago as we walked through the forest, and she just busted it out. God, Rem, she's adorable. She's amazing. She's—"

"Please stop." He was crying now. I could hear it in his voice, and I hated it.

"I'm sorry." Sorry for getting carried away, sorry for making him cry, sorry that he couldn't see how great she was and spend all of his time with her like I could. Mostly I was just sorry he only had Angela, but I had his daughter and I wanted him here with me too. A year and a half apart and I still wanted him more than anything, and talking to him again brought that all back to the surface.

I heard him sniffling. "It's okay. We chose to let your parents raise her and I'm glad she's with you all. It's a good place for her. I'm sure of it."

"You and Angela still good?" I asked him, changing the subject to keep him from crying.

"More or less. We're okay most of the time. College is hard, as I'm sure you know, and sometimes we fight."

That made me frown. "About what?"

"She doesn't miss her like I do. I can't help missing her. Sometimes I just sit there and look at this ultrasound picture of her—it's the only one I have of her—and miss her so much I can't stop crying and have to miss class. Angela will think about her sometimes, but she doesn't get like that. I know we could have had pictures taken while we were there in the hospital and your parents took a few I think, but I didn't get any. I was being stupid about it and I wish I had some, but Angela was so adamant about not wanting any pictures and I didn't want to upset her after everything she'd just been through."

I wiped at my eyes and wished I didn't cry so much around him. He must have thought I was a mess, if he thought about me at all anymore. "Do you want more pictures of her?"

"Can you send them?"

I smiled through my tears. "Yeah. I can send you stuff. Rem, I wish you were here. I wish you could see her."

"Me too. Would you go to lunch with me if I was? Could we go to a movie?"

I would have loved to do those things with him. "Yes. I like pumpkin pie and bacon burgers. Generally in that order, but I'll make an exception for you." I wanted to hold hands with him, to push Madeline along in her muted pastel stroller with him, to do anything with him. "We could go into Denver and go to the zoo or a museum, then get lunch after."

He was smiling now, I was sure of it. "I'd like that. Thomas, I'm sorry, but I need to go."

"Busy?" I asked him.

"No. This just hurts too much. I thought I could talk to you and not miss you too, but I can't miss you and her at the same time and not sit here crying harder than I already am."

I knew exactly what he meant. "I'll send you some pics. Is your e-mail still the same?"

"Yeah."

I already knew which ones I was going to send him. "You don't have to look at them, but they'll be there for you if you ever want to. And Rem, you can call other days of the year too. I can only talk to you about her on her birthday, according to my parents, but if you ever just want to say hi, I'll always take your call."

"I'd like that. Thanks. Will you put a picture of yourself in there with the ones with her? I... I don't have any of you."

"Yeah. I can do that. I miss you." *I still love you.*

"I miss you too." He hung up, and I sighed loudly before coming down the stairs to get another cookie for myself too. I needed at least a handful of them after that conversation.

I HOPED to hear from Rem again soon, but it would be four months before he'd reach out to me. "Thomas! You've got a package!" Mom called me inside. I pulled Madeline off the swing we'd been playing on and carried her inside. She was pretty good at walking, but I still liked carrying her most of the time, especially when we had to cross the little parking lot that was right in front of the row of townhouses.

Mom had already put the package down on the dining room table when I came in, and I helped Madeline into her high chair before sitting down at the table myself. It didn't look like Rem's writing, too curvy and pretty for sure, but with almost two years since the last time I'd seen him, maybe he'd changed his handwriting. I should have known better as I opened the little yellow package and wedding photos spilled out onto the table.

Mom and Dad came over to see what had made me gasp, and she quickly tried to pull them away from me, but I put my hand over hers, stopping her. Of course they'd gotten married. It was practically inevitable. Hot college quarterback with a nearly guaranteed pro football career and the beautiful daughter of a senator. High school sweethearts turned college loves turned married people.

And he was still so amazing looking standing there in his black tux with the beach behind them. I knew that beach and could actually see the rocks I'd gone to when I'd needed time alone. The rocks were sticking out of the right side of the picture of them kissing with the waves behind them and the sun coming down over them. They looked perfect together.

I took out my phone and quickly dialed Rem as I pulled Angela's letter toward me and started reading.

"Hey. What's up? Everything okay with Madeline?" he asked me right away. It was nice to know he cared about her that much and was worried about her.

I swallowed back my hurt and the love I still had for him and tried to be an adult about this. "Yeah. She's good. Right beside me actually. Angela sent me some photos. Looks like you had a really nice wedding." I couldn't stop a little of the hurt from coming through, but I hope he didn't dwell on it. I still loved him; that wasn't going away. I could be a man about him getting married to someone else, though, and try to just be happy for him.

"Shit. I'm sorry. I didn't want you to see them. I didn't want you knowing."

I shook my head and put Angela's letter aside. She wished I could have been there as Rem's best man instead of some guy she didn't really like who was on the Crusaders with him. But she understood I was busy with classes and the baby.

"It's fine," I told him quickly. "You looked good. So did she." Responsible adult, here I came. This wasn't some artsy independent movie I liked to watch between studying where the cute gay guy actually got his man. This was Hollywood, home of the pretty woman and the sexy man coming together and living happily ever after. As good as Rem looked in a tux, I could have never worn a dress, and the movies never went the way they should have for me. I shook my head and tried to slow down my racing thoughts. This being-happy-for-him thing sucked ass.

"Thanks. You sure you're okay?"

I ran a hand over my face. "If I lie to you and say I'm glad you two got married and that leaving Miami was the best choice I ever made, would it make you feel better?" I snapped at him. I had to take a deep breath and get myself under control before I said something I really regretted. "Sorry. I'm sorry. That was unfair, and you didn't deserve it. No, I'm not great. But, Rem, you're not mine. You never were. And I'm glad you get to live the life you want. Please tell Angela how beautiful she looked and thank her for the photos for me. I gotta go."

"No you don't. You just want to go away."

I rolled my eyes. "Then let me go. I'm not yours either, so you don't get to make me do anything, including stay on the phone with you."

He laughed, and that sound managed to make me smile just a little. "Sure. Bye, Thomas."

"Bye, Rem." I hung up on him and turned to look over at Madeline. "Okay, Cutie. What should we do with these photos of my ex and his wife?"

"Burn them," Dad suggested. "Always burn photos of exes. It's the only way to get rid of the feelings."

I snorted and shook my head. "Why, Madeline, what a big deep voice you have there. And so many new words." Dad laughed from the kitchen behind me. "Want to make some cookies with me, Cutie?"

She clapped her hands together and grinned at me. "Cookies!"

"There's your answer. Get to it," Mom said. I turned to see her and Dad vacating the kitchen for us. "Dusty! Get down here and help with the cookies!" Mom called up to him.

He pounded down the stairs a few seconds later, and by the time the first batch was in the oven and I was eating more cookie dough than the cookies I put into the oven, I was starting to feel a bit better. Rem had his family but I had mine, and he probably didn't get to make a mess of his kitchen while baking awesome cookies all the time with his.

TWO MONTHS went by without me hearing from Rem. I could have called him, but after finding out that he was married, I figured I should give him some space. So I waited for him to call me. Of course that didn't mean I stopped myself from sending him pictures and videos of Madeline and me. I'd just finished e-mailing him some pictures from the day before of her feeding giraffes at a zoo in Colorado Springs when he called me.

"Is there seriously a giraffe's tongue around her hand?" he asked me.

I laughed and sent him a few more of her and a wallaby. "Hello to you too, Rem. Check your e-mail for some more pictures. She had a blast at the zoo yesterday."

"She's getting so big."

I smiled down at my laptop and scrolled through my pictures of her. "Yeah she is." Dusty came into the room, and I wanted to keep talking to Rem and get some privacy so I went outside to the park and sat down on the bench facing the townhouse. "How's life for you?"

"Decent. Lots of practices and games and getting ready for pro coaches and making sure I look good for them. What's that weird mini kangaroo thing she's petting? Is it dangerous?"

"Hope not since I petted it too. It's a wallaby." I liked hearing the worry in his voice. "You always look good."

He snickered. "You always seemed to think so, but I don't think you were ever right." He was quiet for a moment, and I listened to the sound of him breathing and thought about when we would lie together in our dorm room at night and I'd feel his breath on my neck. "Are you seeing anyone?" he asked me.

"Nope." I'd considered it, even gone on a few dates here and there. But they weren't him, and it wasn't the same for me.

"Because of Madeline?" He sounded worried, like somehow being part-time caregiver of a toddler would take away all my free time. He was only half-wrong there, though.

I shook my head. "No. Not because of her." I let him think whatever he wanted to. The time away from him had given me some perspective, especially when it came to the realization that yeah, he wasn't ever going to be an out bisexual quarterback and be openly mine, but it hadn't made me care about him any less.

"Do you get the college football games on TV there?" he asked, changing the subject a few seconds later.

"Sure. Local ones. Not Miami, though. I've looked."

"You were trying to watch me play?" he asked me.

There was an implication of caring there, but of course I cared about him. "Little bit. But like I said, we don't get the games here."

"Can I send you a clip of the highlights from the games? The coaches make them so we can show our families if they can't make it to them. They're short and not the best quality, though. Fair warning."

I smiled as I thought about being able to look at him again, even if it was just in a highlight video. "Sure. I'd like that."

"I'll e-mail you a few."

He was quiet for a bit, and I leaned back and let the sun warm my face. Early spring in Colorado had weird weather shifts between days in the seventies and snow two days later. "Do you want to talk about Madeline at all?" I asked him.

"Her birthday's not for another few months," he reminded me.

I nodded. I knew how old she was and that she'd be turning two that summer. "Yeah, but I don't think my parents would mind. I'm not spilling national secrets here or anything. So, if you want to talk about her, we can."

"Thank you. I think about her all the time. She was tiny when she was born."

91

I smiled, remembering. "I was afraid to hold her at first. And when I did, I kept seeing you in her face and the color of her eyes. It was hard to deal with for a few months."

"I wish you'd been there when she was born. I would have liked to share that with you. I know why you weren't, though."

"Because it would have been too hard." I would have been hurting too much, and I would have cried at not being able to hold him when he had to let Madeline go. I'd seen the pictures of him holding her. I knew how much he'd wanted to keep her in that moment because I'd seen his face. And I would have done anything to keep him from hurting like that.

"Yeah…."

I heard him sigh and imagined him sitting there, looking miserable. Actually, I needed a little help picturing him. "Are you still in the dorm room we had?" I asked him.

"Nope. Once we got married Angela's dad bought us a condo. It's a few blocks from school, and I can see the ocean from the living room. The senator likes showing off his money I guess. I could have gotten a job or something, she could have too, but I guess it's so much easier having daddy's money around."

He didn't sound all that happy about it, and I winced at the resentment I could hear in his voice. "Hey, she loves you remember? Be nice."

Rem laughed a little, but there was nothing happy about the sound. "You shouldn't have to tell me to be nice when I talk about my wife and her family. That's just sad."

"Then don't give me a reason to say it. Tell me what color your walls are instead and what you're doing right now. If you're sitting on something." I didn't like thinking about their wedding pictures, but they helped me picture him. "You cut your hair for the wedding."

"I did. It was supposed to look more polished."

I moved over to the swing set so I could swing and drag my feet through the little pebbles while we talked. "I miss touching your curls. Remember the nights I fell asleep with my fingers in your hair?"

"I do. I miss them. I miss you too."

I nodded and hung my head as I kicked the little pebbles around. "I miss you too."

"The walls are this light blue color. I'm sitting on the couch that faces the balcony and the ocean. The couch is white. The floors are a light wood."

I licked my lips as I thought about him. I'd missed his birthday and didn't even know when it was. I might have missed more than one of them. "When's your birthday anyway? We never got around to that."

He laughed a little. "Christmas, actually. I mostly just ignore it, though. Everyone else did while I was growing up, for the most part."

I groaned and shook my head. "That sounds awful. So you didn't get double presents or anything like that?"

"Nope. Nothing like that. It's really not a big deal. When's yours?"

The last time I'd seen him, it had been right before his birthday. I shook my head and wished I'd known. "July first. You should have said something to me, though, when you were here. We could have done something special for your birthday before you went back to Miami."

He chuckled, and I heard something shift under him. Maybe he was lying on the couch or something. "I did get something special for my birthday."

I frowned, trying to remember what was different that we did, but then I figured it was probably something Angela did for him and I suddenly didn't want to know because my best guess was that it had been something sexual.

"You're quiet," he said, and I could hear the smile in his voice.

Shrugging, I got up from the swing and went back to the bench as some kids walked into the park, and I didn't want to take up the swing with my moping if they wanted to use it. "Yeah. Just not really wanting to know what Angela did to you for your birthday. I'm okay with you being married and knowing that she's going to be a permanent part of your life, but some things are just hard for me to handle."

He was laughing now, and I had no idea what was so funny. "What?" I asked him.

"Oh wow, you're dense sometimes. You. I got you for my birthday. We went into the woods by your house, we kissed, I turned you around…. Any of this sounding familiar yet?"

I blushed deeply and looked down at my feet. "Yeah. I think I remember that." I hadn't been able to think about anything else for weeks after he'd gone home.

"So do I. I miss you."

I was about to ask him if he just missed the sex, but there was no way to make that sound teasing like I would have wanted it to sound with my mom coming out of the townhouse toward me. "I miss you too. I think I need to go. My mom's looking at me like I forgot to do something again."

"I gotta go too. Angela should be getting out of her evening class soon, and I promised to start the laundry."

I smiled thinking about him doing laundry. Actually, thinking about him at all made me smile. When I wasn't hurting at least. "Bye."

"Talk to you later."

I hung up the phone and got up to meet my mom. "Hi."

"Rem?" she asked me.

I nodded. "Yeah."

She gave me a little smile and patted my shoulder. "He's a good boy." I was surprised she thought that about him, given she knew he'd been cheating on his then girlfriend with me. "Come inside for an after-school snack. We're having celery and peanut butter."

I made a face. "I'm a little old for an after-school snack. And I don't even leave the house to go to school."

She shrugged and looped her hand through my arm, bringing me back to the house. "You can watch Dusty and try to keep him out of trouble for a few minutes, then. I need to make some desserts for the diner, but my hands are acting up again so it might take me a little longer than usual. It would be nice to have him occupied so I could concentrate."

"Or you could relax and take care of your arthritis and let us make some cookies and brownies for the diner," I offered.

She gave me a look, like she wasn't sure if I could handle it, but Madeline and I made cookies all the time, and Dusty wasn't completely useless if you promised him the spoons so he could lick them off. "We'll be fine," I assured her. Did I want to spend my evening baking desserts for customers at the diner to buy? Not especially. But I wanted to help my mom out, and besides, it wasn't like I had a whole lot else to do. My classes were basically about checking in twice a week, and other than that I didn't have to do much at all.

"Okay. If you're sure."

"I am." We went back into the house, and I lifted Madeline off the couch where she'd been watching a sitcom with Dad and took her to the kitchen where she could sit on the counter next to me.

"What we do?" she asked me as she sucked at her thumb.

I gently pulled her thumb out of her mouth and used a baby wipe to clean her hands. "We're making cookies. And try not to suck your thumb. Dusty, you're helping."

He plodded over and got up on the counter next to Madeline. Mom didn't like him up there, but if it got him to cooperate and do something productive, I wasn't going to make him get down. "Do I have to?" he whined.

I pulled the sugar, flour, and butter out onto the island where they couldn't knock them off. "Cookies or homework? Your choice."

"Cookies," he told me instantly.

I grinned at him, and he looked slightly less resigned to such a horrible fate. "That's what I thought." I looked over our haul and chewed on my bottom lip as I considered our options. "Okay, gang, peanut butter, peanut butter chocolate chip, double chocolate chip, sugar, or snickerdoodles. What's your pick?"

"All," Dusty said, surprising me.

"Madeline, lots of cookies sound good to you too?" I asked her.

She clapped her hands together and squealed, "Cookies!" sealing our evening. Laughing, I got down to it and started helping Dusty measure flour for the first batch of cookies. It wasn't a half-bad way to spend a few hours, actually.

"EVERYONE LOVED your cookies," Mom told me a few days later after coming back from her shift at the diner.

I looked up from where I was answering some questions for my chemistry class on my laptop. Dusty was across from me eating a PB and J and Madeline was enjoying juice from her sippy cup while Dad worked out back. It was a normal Friday morning for me, and I liked it.

"That's good," I said, not looking up from the screen.

"You have orders."

That did make me turn to look at her as she put a slip of paper in front of me with cookie orders and the names and phone numbers of people I'd known for years that were, for some reason I didn't really understand, wanting to order cookies from me using the same recipes that I'd always known.

"Uh." I picked up the piece of paper and really looked at it this time. "You tell these eight people that I'm not really a baker?"

She snorted and ruffled my hair. "Thornwood people apparently like your cookies. Better get to making them."

I laughed and quickly finished my assignment—a tiny two-hundred-word post on what I thought about glycerin, which wasn't much, but whatever, I could fake a few hundred words—and headed into the kitchen.

"Cookies?" Madeline asked me when I started pulling out the ingredients and also making a list of the things we'd need before I could make too many batches.

I glanced up at her and nodded. "Yeah, baby, cookies. You want to help?" She grinned at me, and I went over to grab her so she could join me in the kitchen.

"Dusty?" I offered him.

"Busy!"

Rolling my eyes, I pulled out Mom's recipe book with Madeline still on my hip, and we went through the old pages together trying to find new recipes to try. I liked making cookies with her, and soon we moved into brownies and bars.

CHAPTER ELEVEN

BY THE time Rem called me on Madeline's second birthday, we were going strong with lots of orders each week. Apparently Thornwood people liked eating cookies made with the help of a two-year-old.

"Hey, Maddie's Cookies," I said as I answered my phone, expecting even more orders for the week though we were already swamped.

"Cookies!" Madeline cried from the background where I had her taste testing chocolate cheesecake bites at the table.

"Uh, hey."

I sighed and folded myself over the island. "Oh thank God it's you and not more of these people wanting cookies. This town has gone crazy," I told Rem.

"Dramatic child, enough of your whining," Mom called down to me.

"I also need to find my own place," I grumbled. "Hey."

"You sound busy. Should I call back later?" he asked me.

I shook my head and got comfortable at the table next to Madeline. "Nope. Now's good. How's things there? Miami as horrible in June as it was in August?"

He laughed. "Yeah. It's miserable. I spent most of the day in the pool." Of course he did. I groaned just thinking about him in there, all wet, in just a little bit of clothing. Or nothing at all.

"What wrong?"

I looked over at Madeline to see her watching me intently. "Nothing, Cutie. Eat your cookie, and tell me if it's good enough to sell."

"Is that her? Was that her talking?"

I realized that, even though she'd been talking sometimes in the background when I talked to Rem, he'd probably never heard her all that clearly before. I could hear the anxiety in his voice, like he could barely breathe, and I smiled. "Yeah, Rem. That's Madeline."

"Can I talk to her? I mean, would it be okay with your parents?"

I wanted to say yes, of course he could talk to her. But he was right to wonder if Mom and Dad were okay with it. They were her parents, not me. "One second. Let me ask."

"Okay."

I put him on mute and went in search of Mom and Dad. I found them in the living room watching an old black and white movie. I leaned over the back of the couch so I could look at them both. "Hey. Rem's on the phone. I muted it so that he can't hear us right now. But he wants to talk to Madeline. You two okay with that?"

Dad didn't look concerned, but Mom wasn't too happy about it as she frowned at me. "I think that will be fine, but you don't think he'll try to get custody of her now, do you?"

Well, that came out of left field. "Nope. She's legally yours. I think he just wants to say hi. He's never talked to her before."

She nodded, just a little, though. "Okay. But keep him on speakerphone. And tell him not to confuse her. She's only two for Christ's sake."

"Yep. Will do." I took him off mute as I headed into the kitchen. "Hey. You there?"

"Yeah. You need to figure out how to mute your phone." He didn't sound that happy anymore.

"Well, shit," I mumbled, far too softly for anyone else in the house to hear me. "You okay?"

"Your mom really thinks I'd try to take her?"

I leaned back against the wall and shrugged. "I guess she might. You obviously care about her. Maybe when you get to a point in your life that you could care for her, you would." He sighed, and I gripped my phone a little harder. "Don't be mad. Don't go. Don't hang up so soon." I was probably begging, but it didn't matter to me. I just wanted him to stay with me a little while longer. I didn't call him because it didn't feel right calling him just to say hi given everything we'd been through, and I'd been looking forward to talking to him for months.

"I'm not going anywhere," he promised me. "I just wish I could make your mom see that I didn't want to try to steal her from you. She belongs there. I've seen the pictures and videos you've sent me. I've saved every single one of them. I know how happy she is with you and your parents. I'd never do that to her." He groaned, and I nodded. "Damn, now I'm crying."

I smirked. I was too, and it sucked that I cried so easily around him when I hardly ever even got sad when it had nothing to do with him. "Me too."

"Could I talk to her? Just for a little while. Speakerphone is fine."

I wanted them to talk, and I started heading back to Madeline so I could sit down next to her. "Yes. You can. Just, Rem, don't tell her about you being her dad. I'll say you're my friend from college."

"Is that what your mom meant about me confusing her?"

"Yeah." I sat down next to Madeline. "That okay with you?"

"I won't say anything."

I had to trust him in this, but I realized doing so wasn't all that hard for me. I put the phone on speaker, which I did know how to do, thank you very much techno gods, and turned to Madeline, who was watching me with her big green eyes and chocolate stains all over her face. "Apparently you liked that cookie, huh?"

She nodded to me. "More."

"Not yet. First, my friend, Rem, from college would like to say hi to you. Okay?"

"Then cookie?"

There was no way she was getting another one so soon. "Maybe. Say hi."

She leaned forward and tried to grab my phone out of my hands, but I'd learned the hard way chocolate wasn't great for phones, so I pulled it out of her reach. "Hi, Rem!" she squealed into it.

"Hey, Madeline. So… you're eating cookies?"

"Lots of cookies."

I tried not to laugh and wondered what Rem thought of me giving her "lots" of cookies to eat. "It's been like two. Maybe two and a half," I told him.

"Hey, I'm not judging. I like cookies."

She was grinning, and I wished Rem could have been there with her talking instead of a thousand or so miles away and over the phone. "Me too," Madeline said. "Potty!"

"Uh-oh," I said as she reached for me.

"You gotta go?" Rem asked me.

But my mom was already getting up from the couch to come get her. "Nope, Mom's taking her." I took him off speakerphone as Mom came over and took Madeline upstairs after ruffling my hair and giving me what I figured had to be a relieved smile. "Sorry that was so short," I said when they were gone.

"It's fine… It was good. She sounds great. And happy. Really, really happy. Thank you for that. Seriously, Thomas. Thanks for letting me talk to her. I needed that." He was crying again, I could hear it in his voice, and I laid my chin down over my arm on the table.

"Of course. And she is happy. Oh, before I forget, Maddie's Cookies, how I answered the phone, she's a mini entrepreneur. Thornwood folks love her cookies and other random sweets, and they sell them at the diner right by the cash register. Most days they can't keep enough of them in stock to last until dinner, and we get a bunch of orders during the week too. I think this town's gone crazy, but she seems happy doing it." And I was seriously proud of her for being able to stand all of the attention when we made runs to go drop off more of the sweets and people started kissing on her.

He chuckled, and I wished I could have seen his smile. I would have sat on his lap, put my arms around his shoulders, and smiled right back down at him. Then I would have kissed him until neither one of us could breathe. "Child labor there, huh?" I could tell he was joking, and it made me laugh.

"Hey, college is damn expensive now. I hope to have my loans paid off by the time I'm forty." That wasn't an exaggeration, either. And her college fund was right where the profits went.

"Are you back in school?"

I watched Mom take Madeline into her room to lay her down for a nap and knew some screaming would be coming as she settled in. To avoid it I got up and went outside to go sit on the front step and talk to him for as long as I could. "Yeah. I started online at a university in Denver as soon as I was back here. Going for business now instead of general stuff. I don't love it but maybe it'll come in handy someday. What's new with you?"

"Angela and I aren't doing so well. We're fighting a lot, and we started seeing a marriage counselor."

I flinched. "I'm sorry. That sucks."

"You aren't even a little happy about it?"

That was an awful thing to say, but I could kind of understand where he was coming from. "Even if you weren't with her, you'd never be mine. Not really anyway."

"Because I won't be out?"

I nodded and wished I could get him to change his mind. "Yep."

"I'm sorry."

"Don't be. You have your reasons. And they aren't bad ones. I just can't live like that. I want you to be with her, to make things work. You both deserve the Hollywood ending."

"And what about you? What do you deserve?" he asked me, and I didn't really know.

I shrugged. "Something else. I'll figure it out."

"I miss you. I think about you all the time."

Smiling, I got up to head back into the house since I couldn't hear Madeline crying out anymore. "I miss you too."

"Talk soon?"

"Yeah." We hung up after that, and I tried to focus on the cookie orders, but I just couldn't do it. So instead I gave in and did what I wanted to anyway. I watched the videos Rem had sent me of his game highlights. If I was going to spend a few hours thinking about him,

I figured I might as well have sat in my bed watching the videos I'd watched a hundred times before.

I missed him, and the videos helped a little, but they didn't replace the memories I had of being next to him. Nothing was as good as that.

REM WAITED nearly a year to call me again, and I was a bit angry about that, but really, what was I supposed to do? I'd decided not to call him, to let him call me if he wanted to talk, a long time before that. He caught me in the middle of painting my new living room in my new townhouse. It wasn't really new, since they were about thirty years old, but it was mine, and I'd only lived in it a week, but I loved every inch of it.

"Hey," I said, already smiling once I'd seen his number.

"Hey. You busy?"

I put the paint roller in the tray, tried not to step in pale yellow paint, and shook my head. "Nope. What's up with you?"

"I wanted to invite you out to see me graduate."

I still had another year left, but then I remembered Rem was a year older than me when I'd started. "You're already done? I thought your first semester of Miami College was with me."

"It was. But I spent a year at Tallahassee Community before coming down to Miami. So now I'm done. And I'd like you here so we can celebrate together before the draft happens and I find out if I get picked for the pros or not. Please say you'll come. Please?"

His offer was tempting—oh so much so. To actually be able to hold him, to kiss him, to.... There would be none of that, I realized. And knowing that made me shake my head. "I can't. I'm sorry."

"Because you're busy?" He didn't sound happy about me saying no.

I snorted and shook my head as I tried to find a place to sit. I hadn't brought over any of my furniture, not that I had all that much, so the only place I had was either a paint can or the counter. I chose the counter. "I'm never too busy for you. I don't want to have to stand there and see you so close after all these years and not be able to touch you or kiss you."

"I want my best friend there to celebrate with me," he pushed.

"And I want to be able to kiss the man I gave my virginity to." I could be a pushy prick when I wanted to be. That wasn't his exclusive right.

He chuckled. "Yeah. Okay. That's fair. So how's things with you?"

It was nice not to be in that loop with him again. I couldn't see him. As much as I wanted to, that just wasn't going to happen. "Good. Bought a townhouse two doors down from my parents. It's a rent to own, and the guy that used to own it smoked cigars, so it needs to air out some, but it's mine, and I don't have to share my room with Dusty."

"Nice. Hey, I never asked, and it's not my business, but what's the deal with Dusty?"

"Huh?" I had no idea what he was getting at.

"Are your parents adopting him? Fostering?"

"Oh." Okay, well he was making much more sense now. "Fostering. His mom is going through this messy court thing, and it keeps getting pushed back and rescheduled. My parents would love to adopt him, but while there's still a chance of her getting him back, they won't be able to."

"Ah. I was just curious. Sorry if it really wasn't my business. Should have asked that first."

I shrugged. I didn't really care. "No problem."

"Hey… are you alone right now?"

"Yeah."

His voice had changed a little bit, and the difference made me shiver because I remembered that tone. He'd last used it with me in the woods. "I'm going to e-mail you a video. Watch it when you're alone. But preferably with me right now."

"Okay…." I opened it when it came into my e-mail and instantly knew why he wouldn't want anyone else seeing a video of his cock. "Rem, I don't want to watch something you made for Angela," I quickly said. Didn't mean I wasn't going to watch it. I hadn't exactly lied, and seeing Rem's dick again instantly brought my own cock to life.

"I didn't. You think I'd send you secondhand porn? No. God no. I like you way more than that. Turn the sound up on the video."

I did and was instantly blushing. *"Fuck I miss you, Thomas. Your mouth, so wet as I slid into you. I seriously did not think you were a virgin after getting head like that. No way you could have been."*

He was stroking himself on the video as he talked to me, and I slid off the counter so that I could put the phone down on it and lean my forearm down. I was so very glad I'd worn comfortable shorts with an elastic waistband that morning as I pushed them down my hips and took myself out.

"Shit. When did you make this?"

Rem laughed. "This morning. I woke up hard and thinking about you."

I shook my head and stroked myself just as he did on the video.

"What are you doing?" he asked me.

"What do you think?" I grumbled at him. "You can't send me a cock video and not expect me to get down to it. Fuck I miss you."

I heard him undo a zipper. "Wait a second, I'll come with you."

This violated a lot of the rules I'd made for myself once Rem and Angela had gotten married, but I couldn't really make myself care right then either. "I'm in my kitchen, leaning over the counter," I told him, giving him a visual.

"Just like a dryer," he reminded me, making it impossible for me not to think of our first time together.

I licked my lips and slowed my hand. "Yeah. Your fingertips digging into my hip. Your hand on my shoulder."

"My cock in your ass."

I shook with his words and lowered my head. "God, Rem...."

"I know." He sounded like he was getting breathless too. "I hear your voice and I'm instantly hard. I'd love to make this last, but I can't."

I knew exactly what he meant. I was trying to hang on, to hold off on my own orgasm, but my body was fighting me, and it wasn't going to work out in my favor. Watching him come on the video was my undoing, and I groaned as I sprayed against the cabinets.

"Fuck. Thomas. I didn't know you sounded like that," he gasped out.

I chuckled breathlessly. "We were never in a place where we could make any noise."

He gasped my name when he came, and I closed my eyes as I savored that sound. He had never done it before, and it hurt that I couldn't have him with me when he came while thinking about me.

"Thank you."

"You always say that," I told him with a smile.

He laughed a little. "Yeah, and I always mean it. Wish I could put my mouth over your cock and clean you up."

"Wish we could take a shower together too," I said.

"Someday we will."

It was a promise he couldn't make, but I didn't say that. I knew there wouldn't be a time like that for us. It was better just to keep it like this between us. I loved him, I hadn't stopped, and I wanted him with everything I had. But he wasn't mine to have or to want, and that call became just another stolen moment between us.

ANGELA MISSED Madeline's third birthday, but Rem called me right after 2:00 p.m.

"Hey, I can't talk long, but I wanted to say hi."

I smiled because I knew exactly why he couldn't talk. "Draft's today. Madeline and I are watching it already. Good luck." I handed over some popcorn for her to munch on while I got off my couch to go get a bottle of water.

"You are?"

I didn't know why he sounded so surprised by that. "Yeah. Of course we are. We're sitting in my townhouse on my couch watching it right now. Well, she's sitting. I had to get up for some more water.

If you were here, instead of about to find out what team you'll be playing for, you'd get to have some popcorn with us. The anticipation of which animal you'll have on your helmet is killing us."

"Ha-ha. You're such a jackass. God, I miss you."

I plopped down next to Madeline. "Miss you too. Hey, why'd you take a year at a community college when these guys on the TV make you sound like such a big deal?" They were even making a stink about how he'd gone to Miami College instead of some Ivy League school. "Didn't know you were some superstar football guy."

He laughed, and I heard people talking in the background. "I wasn't, not really. When I was a quarterback, I was second string and benched a lot of the time. They moved me to receiving tight end in my junior year, and the position fit a lot better for me. Now I guess I'm something special. That's what they tell me anyway. Tell Madeline hi for me please. And happy birthday. I gotta get going. Wish me luck."

"I already did that," I reminded him, but I was smiling. I leaned over to Madeline. "Honey, say hi to Rem. He's going to be on TV soon."

"Hi, Rem!" she practically screamed into the phone.

I laughed, and I heard Rem laughing too. "I gotta go," he said, sounding very much like he didn't want to.

"Go get signed with someone," I told him.

"I'd rather stay and talk to you."

I wanted that too. "Call when you can."

"I wish I had longer to talk to you both."

I wished he did too. "Go on. You've gotta go."

"Yeah. See you."

"Bye."

It wasn't more than twenty minutes after we'd hung up that Madeline and I watched him become an Oregon Kraken. "He looks like he has a squid on his head with that cap on," I said as I shook my head. I started laughing until the camera panned over to where Rem and Angela were kissing off to the side of the stage.

"Ew...," Madeline said as she cringed back.

"Yeah. Very ew. Yucky germs. Huh?" I asked her.

She nodded at me. "Yep."

After that I changed the channel and put it back on cartoons for her. I didn't need to see the man I loved kissing his wife, and Madeline had no idea what was going on. It had been good to see him, though. To see him smiling and looking happy again. Even if it wasn't with me.

"Cutie, you want to go buy some stuff for your room in a little bit?" I asked her.

"Yeah."

Good. It was settled, then. I had a job at the grocery store, but I didn't make all that much. So I didn't have many things in my townhouse yet, but Madeline had her own room for when she fell asleep while she was hanging out with me. We ate on the couch and I slept on a cheap mattress. But it was mine, and it was so fucking great to have some quiet for a little while and a place to get away where no one just burst into my room.

It hadn't been all bad living at home. It hadn't been bad at all actually. But I hadn't realized how much I liked a bit of quiet time until I had my own place. Now it felt like a big deal whenever Dusty came running in, whereas before it would have just been a normal part of life.

CHAPTER TWELVE

REM CALLED me again six months later. And it wasn't with good news. "Hey. Angela and I are getting a divorce," he told me before I could even say hi. I sat down heavily on my bed. I'd been in the middle of putting my laundry away.

"I'm sorry." I tried to figure out how he felt about it, but I really couldn't decide from the way he sounded. He didn't seem all that upset, though. Which I thought was weird.

"It's fine. I'll be moving into an apartment soon. Her dad bought the condo. It doesn't make sense that she'd have to move out. And I need to be in Oregon soon anyway. She'd never be okay in Oregon."

"Yeah. I guess." I frowned. "You don't sound all that upset. You really that okay with it?"

He laughed, though there was no happiness in the sound. More like he was angry. "I told her, Thomas. I told her about being bi, about cheating on her with guys while we were together."

My heart was racing. He'd really done it? Seriously? "Including me?"

"No. Not with you. She doesn't know anything about us. I just couldn't do it anymore. She was talking about trying to have kids once we got to Oregon, and I couldn't talk to her about it anymore. Not when she stopped saying Madeline's name before she even turned two."

"She didn't call last year." I'd checked with my mom to make sure since she hadn't mentioned it, and Mom had been pretty upset that Angela would skip Madeline's birthday completely.

Rem sighed. "I know. She said she forgot. How do you just forget something like that?"

Shrugging, I didn't understand it either. "So…. Oregon? And a divorce?" That was a lot to go through.

"I want you to come visit me. When I'm settled in, when I've got a place. I want you here."

That was really fast for me. Of course I wanted to see him, but I hadn't been around him in four years. "What about your career? Will Angela out you?"

"No. I'm paying her a decent percentage of my contract for the next three years. After that we negotiated for the percentage to go down, but as long as I'm playing pro football and she keeps my secret, she'll get part of what I make each year."

He didn't sound happy about that, but I wouldn't have been either. "Ouch."

"Yeah. Not great. But it did seem fair when I saw how upset she was by knowing I'd been cheating on her off and on for years. It sucks, but she deserved better than I gave her."

I frowned as I thought I understood what he was saying, and it bothered me more than it really should have. "You were with guys after me."

He was quiet for a long moment. "Yes. Weren't you?"

"No." I hadn't been at all, and it hurt a bit that he had. I'd taken care of Madeline, I'd gotten my degree, I had a job at the grocery store…. And I realized right then that those were all excuses, and I could have had sex with anyone I wanted to in that time. I could have met someone, had a relationship with them. I could have even fallen in love with someone new. But I was already in love, and the guy I loved had been with other men since me, as if I hadn't really mattered all that much at all. That's what it felt like to me anyway. "I need a minute."

"Thomas…."

I shook my head. "No. Rem. Just no. Stop for just a second." My free hand was shaking, and I pressed it in a fist against my stomach to get it to stop. "I love you," I whispered to him.

"And I love you too."

He didn't. He couldn't, as far as I was concerned. There was a huge difference between having sex with his wife and having sex with his wife plus whatever guys he'd brought into his bed while I'd loved him for the past four years.

"I have to go."

"Don't. Thomas, come on. Talk to me about this. Why are you so upset? Did you really expect me not to have sex with any other guy after you? It's been years."

He sounded a little desperate to keep me on the phone, and I knew I needed to talk to him, but this was too much to process with him in my ear. I could try, though. I didn't want to stop talking to him and lose another few months without him. "Did any of them mean anything to you?"

"No. Never. It was just sex. Nothing like what we had."

And what did we have? We were just sex in a dorm room and in a laundry room when we both had masks on. It was ridiculous that I was so upset over him being with other people. It shouldn't have mattered. I shouldn't have even asked. "It's fine," I choked out.

"It's not. I can tell that you're still hurting. Come to Oregon. Please? We can talk there. We'll go out to dinner. It'll be good. Please say you'll come out. I'll buy your ticket to get you out there faster. Just give me a week to get a place set up."

Wow he was eager. It felt good to have him want me as much as he seemed to, and part of me thought that maybe seeing him would make everything all better, that maybe it wouldn't be such a big deal that he'd been with other guys while I'd been practically pining away for him. For years. Like some pathetic spinster or something. "You don't have to buy my ticket, though."

"Thomas, I just signed a multimillion dollar deal. Let me be good to you? Please?"

"Okay." Four years apart and it was still so easy to give in to him.

TWO WEEKS later I was off for a few days from my job managing the grocery store and heading to Oregon. I tried to sleep on the flight, but that wasn't happening. I was too excited, too eager, and definitely needing to see him. When I got off the plane and headed to baggage claim to meet him, I wanted to jump into his arms and hug him as tightly as I could. I was nervous, my hands were shaking, and I just could not stop smiling. But when I got close to him, he held out his hand for me to shake, and I realized we were still pretending to just be friends when we were out in public. It dimmed my view of the weekend a bit, but I guess I should have known better. After all, he wasn't out.

He held my hand for longer than was probably appropriate, given that we were two straight guys saying hi in an airport, but I wanted to cling to that contact all the same.

"Hey," I said. He'd always been a bit taller than me at just over six feet, but he'd filled out considerably since college. And fuck he looked good with all that muscle.

He let go of my hand and gave me a smile. "Hi. So… dinner?"

"I'd like to get freshened up back at your place first." That was supposed to sound innocent. Like maybe I'd just spent the last six hours in airports and tiny seats surrounded by strangers. But I saw the wink he gave me, and I knew he understood exactly what I was saying.

We didn't touch as we headed toward his car, which was a sleek sedan that cost a lot by the looks of it. But he was a pro football star now, and I'm sure he could afford it. I wanted to kiss him as soon as we were secluded behind his tinted windows, but when I turned to him, he shook his head.

"Not yet," he said, laying a hand on my inner thigh. He gave me a squeeze, and I opened my thighs for him, letting him know he could touch me wherever he wanted to as he blasted the air conditioning around us and drove me through unfamiliar streets. He kept his hand right where it was, though, with his fingers pressed tightly into my thigh.

"You look good," he said as he pulled up to a condo building with a man in a suit standing by the curb and another holding the front door open for us before he'd even stopped the car. He let go of me before we pulled up to the valet and I nodded.

"So do you." It was all we'd said up to that point. Maybe I couldn't figure out what to say, now that I had him with me. My brain felt like mush, and I could hardly focus past the need I felt rushing through me at the sight of him. Had he always affected me like this? Where I couldn't make a complete thought because all I wanted was him? Maybe that had always been our way, and I just couldn't remember because it had been so long since I'd last seen him in person.

He waved to the guy at the door and tipped the man that took his car. And all the while I couldn't stop staring at him. Four years apart and he'd changed a lot from what I could see. But it wasn't just that his hair had stayed short or that he was growing a lot more stubble on his face or the amount of muscle he'd grown. It was how easy his smile was now, how confident he looked.

We stayed apart in the elevator, and I was careful to look like I was just his straight friend visiting from out of town. Not his gay lover who couldn't wait to be under him again. No, not that at all. Nope.

All that changed once we were alone in his condo and the door was locked behind us, though. I was quick to kick off my shoes as he stepped away from me. "Kitchen's over there, living room, balcony. Oh, you should see this painting I found a few days ago. It's hideous, but for some reason I like it. And—"

I took his hand and pulled him back to me. "Rem, I'll see it later. But right now, and I'm not at all sorry about this, I really don't care because I want you too fucking much."

He grinned at me and crushed his mouth against mine. It was good to have my arms around his shoulders again, to have his hands squeezing my butt through the comfortable shorts I'd worn. He lifted me up, something I never thought someone would ever do to me, and he made it seem so effortless as he carried me over to the couch. The bed would have been more romantic, probably, but the couch was closer, and I didn't need romance for the first time. I just needed him.

I shucked my shirt off, and I was pretty sure I pulled some buttons off in my hurry to get his open as well. Why he'd worn a button-down and nice slacks to come see me, I had no idea. I'd been comfortable in a T-shirt and shorts that were easy to get on and more importantly easy to get off. He pulled them down, and they fell to the floor next to my shirt. In four years I'd gained a little weight and a little muscle too, from carrying Madeline around, along with those heavy bags of flour and sugar all the time, but I knew I looked mostly the same as I had.

His shirt was undone, and I hadn't even started on his pants, but he just ran his hands down my stomach to rest them on my hips. "I missed you so much."

I nodded. I'd missed him too. I leaned up and put my hand behind his head, bringing him back to me for a kiss that felt so good, so right, I wondered how I'd lived without it for so long. He slipped off his shirt while I still had his mouth against mine. He tried to turn me over while his pants were still mostly on, but I stopped him with a hand on his chest.

"I want to see you," I told him.

He looked worried for a moment. "I've never done that with a guy."

"Never done what? Actually looked at a guy you were fucking?" I asked him.

He nodded, and I shook my head, wondering what the hell that was about but not really wanting to get into it either. "I want you this way, where I can see you. Do that for me?"

He gave me a smile and another kiss before shoving a pillow under my hips. He got off the couch to take his pants off and go get a condom and some lube while I watched him from my back on the couch. It was a bit gratifying that he had to search for them for a minute.

"I know I have some," he called to me from somewhere in the bedroom.

I laughed and took my cock into my right hand, stroking myself gently as I waited for him. A few minutes later, he was back with his hands full of little bottles of lube and some condoms. "Sample packs," he told me when I rolled my eyes. "From people wanting me to endorse their products."

That made me snort, but I wasn't laughing for long as he kissed me roughly and began rubbing his stomach against my cock. "I want you," he said as he pulled away.

"I want you too." God I wanted him. Needed him. Every ounce of me felt like I was crying out for his touch, for his attention. And his damn green eyes sparkled like he knew it too. I reached between his legs to touch his cock and remembered the feeling of it, and the little way he pursed his lips when I squeezed him right around his head.

"Fuck…," he groaned when I did just that. He dipped his hips, pushing himself farther into my hand. "I want to suck you, to take my time with you, but I don't think I'd last. Not with you."

"I don't think I would either. Later, then?"

He smirked at me. "Not that much later. I don't expect you to be able to walk right after this weekend."

Laughing, I knew that I would be perfectly fine with that, and I spread my legs as wide as I could on the couch while he stretched me and got me ready for him. I bit my lip as he pushed his cock inside of me. There was pain, and the stretching of parts of my body that hadn't been used like that in years, but it was so fucking good to have him in me again.

He put his hands on my hips, just as he'd always done, his mouth went to the side of my neck, and I dug my fingers into his shoulders so I could hang on to him as tightly as I wanted to. We fit together just as well as we did in college, if not better this way, and with him above me, I got to feel every drag of his soft hair against my body.

"Thomas… Thomas… Thomas…," he whispered as he thrust into me as hard as he could, as if he knew I could take it and wouldn't break under him.

"I love you," I gasped into his curls.

He moved one of his hands from my hip to cup my cheek. "I love you too," he said, rising above me and holding his mouth over mine. "Always did."

I smiled against his lips. Sex with him was always exactly what I needed, and the fevered pace he took me at on the couch that afternoon was the perfect way to start our weekend together. Coming with him inside of me left me shaking, and he kissed me as our hearts stopped racing and we could breathe normally again.

We did go to dinner at this really nice place where another valet parked his car and the host shook his hand and called him "Mister Daniels."

"Nice place," I said as we were seated in a private little alcove well away from everyone.

He smiled at me. "I'm glad you like it. The guys on the team suggested it when I asked for a recommendation of where to take someone that was nice. Apparently a lot of the guys come here since they don't get bombarded by crazy fans a lot." He was grinning like it might not be such a bad thing for someone to jump up and demand his autograph.

"So...," I began.

"So."

I'd dated, but I realized that this was my first official, actual date out with Rem. The only other one we'd even attempted to try had been interrupted by Angela's pregnancy announcement. Remembering that day made me smile a little because, as awful as that day was, I now got to spend most of my free time with a little girl I absolutely thought was awesome because of it.

"What are you thinking about?" he asked me after a waiter had come with bread and cold water that came in little bottles. He even unscrewed the caps for us before pouring the water into our wine glasses. Or were those fancy water goblets or something? I didn't know, and this really wasn't my kind of place. I thought it was nice, but Rem was wearing another button-down shirt and slacks, I was in good jeans, and my idea of a great time was watching a movie on the couch and eating pizza with a paper napkin across my lap. These napkins looked like they had gold embroidery. It was nearly too pretty to use.

"Remember the last time we tried to have a date?" I asked him, coming back to my previous thoughts and avoiding the swirling-napkin thoughts altogether.

I'd kept my voice low because of course we were two straight guys right then, but he still looked a little wide-eyed at me like he couldn't believe what I'd said. "Thomas…," he warned me, as if he hadn't already made it clear we weren't actually dating. Not in any way we could show anyone anyway.

I rolled my eyes. "Yeah, yeah. I know, Rem. I do know. I get it. But I was thinking about that day and how we'd made plans to cut class and go out."

He looked a little more relaxed now as he nodded. "I remember too. The day I found out Angela was pregnant and everything changed." He frowned as if it hurt to talk about, but then he smiled through it. "Madeline okay? What's she doing now?"

Madeline was absolutely a safe topic we could talk about in public, and I put my elbows on the table so that I could lean closer to him while we talked. "She's good. Crazy sometimes. I guess four-year-olds get like that, though. She's currently going through an 'I hate everything that happens to be even a little bit pink' stage right now. Which means that she pretty much got all new clothes last weekend."

I shrugged. I was used to going through clothes with her all the time. She outgrew stuff, destroyed it, or just plain decided that she hated it nearly weekly, but Rem was looking at me like I'd said something strange. "What?"

"You give up a lot for her."

"Not really. And whatever I do give up, it's not that big of a deal to me. She makes me happy, and as weird as it is to like hanging out with a little girl and watching *Penguin Adventures* over and over again—" He looked like he had no idea what I was talking about. "You do know what *Penguin Adventures* is, don't you?"

"Not a clue."

I laughed and shook my head. "You are so lucky. So very, very lucky. It's an animated movie with at least six sequels now, they all come out around Christmas, and they have this catchy music that kids, including Madeline, simply love to sing all day long at the top of their lungs."

He didn't look horrified yet, maybe even mostly intrigued, but if he ever did sit down to watch one of those movies, I was pretty sure he'd know what madness was.

I knew every song by heart, and Madeline had the dance move video that was also a sing-a-long that went with all the movies. It was such a joy. Not.

"I adore her. I really, honestly do. But sometimes I go into my room, put on my headphones, and listen to the loudest, most obnoxious music that I can just to drown out the voices of those damn penguins barging around in my head."

Rem laughed and reached under the table to touch my knee. I put my hand over his and gave his fingers a squeeze.

"Mister Daniels," the waiter said as he came back to us. He gave me a nod as well, and I smiled at him. "Have you and your guest decided on an appetizer? I can come back if you need more time, or do you have any questions about the menu?"

We'd been given menus? Damn, I hadn't even noticed. "Uh…."

Rem rubbed his fingers over my knee, and I blushed. "Sea bass for me, and Thomas?"

It was time to open up the menu and pick something at random. "Lamb and artichokes." Or something like that. The waiter smiled at me, Rem looked happy too, and I was having lamb for dinner. I hadn't even looked at the price when I'd ordered, but now that the waiter was taking back the menus I had a second to glance at it and wow, that was some expensive lamb.

"Rem…."

"Don't even worry about it. Pro football player over here. Remember?"

The waiter walked away, and I focused my attention back on Rem. "You don't have to do this. I would have been fine with pizza. My tastes haven't changed all that much since we were in college."

He chuckled and shook his head. "Mine really haven't either. But it's been four years for us, and I wanted to do something a little nicer. We'll do wings and pizza tomorrow. Or if we're still up at three or something and in desperate need of food."

I smirked because with us and the time we'd spent apart and how much I wanted him, that was a definite possibility. Our food came, and dinner was... well it was lovely. It was stuffy and pretentious with tiny salads and me being afraid to accidentally spill something on my freaking gold embroidered napkin, but it was nice. Mostly because I got to do it with Rem.

We were getting up to leave when someone stopped us, blocking our path and focusing all of his attention on Rem as if I didn't even exist. I was really good with that, though, since the waiters had made me feel like I was on display, and every minute we were, they had to make sure we were taken care of. Great customer service, certainly, but it wasn't something that I was used to.

"Hey," Rem said.

"Hi. I'm Andy, Mister Daniels. I watched the draft, and I'm a big fan of the Kraken. I wanted to wish you luck."

I watched as Rem's face lit up instantly as they shook hands. It was nice to see him get a fan. Maybe it was his first, maybe not, but it was the first one I'd seen him with, and he looked pretty damn happy as he signed one of the napkins for the guy.

"Is this your boyfriend?" Andy asked him.

I was going to deny it, since we were just two friends when we were out. But Rem beat me to it. "No. He's just a friend from college. I'm not a fag."

Fucking hell. Well, then. I had my phone out and was searching flights back home before they'd finished shaking hands again. We left the restaurant with me still on my phone and glaring at the price of what it would cost to leave Oregon tonight, preferably within the next hour or two. It was fucking ridiculous. Fine, then. While the valet brought the car around, I checked hotel prices. I had a few credit cards on me, but none of them had the thousands upon thousands I'd need to leave town available on them.

A hotel I could definitely afford, and I'd booked a room before Rem had even noticed I was currently not speaking to his lying, judgmental, homophobic ass. "You okay?" he asked me as he started up his car and began heading out, probably back to his condo, where he likely thought I was going to strip off my clothes and we could have sex nice and slowly this time. That had been my plan up until the last minutes of dinner. There was no way that was happening now.

"Perfectly fine. For a fag." I turned and glared at him. "Don't you ever say that word around me again."

"Thomas…. C'mon. It didn't mean anything. It's just a word. I had to show him that I wasn't gay."

He tried to reach over and touch my thigh, but I pushed his hand away. "No. You don't get to touch me right now. Take me back to your condo. Call me a taxi while I pack, and next time you want to talk about Madeline, call my mother. I don't want to hear from you again."

"What the hell?" he snapped at me. We stopped fighting while he pulled up in front of his building, and yet another valet came and took his car away, and the nice man at the door smiled at us both, and the elevator music played on, and by the time we got into his condo I was so full of pent-up anger that I had to get away from him before I said something I might have really regretted.

I packed in silence, angrily tossing my clothes into my backpack, which was all I'd brought with me since I was only staying the weekend, and when he came to the doorway a few minutes later, I was ready to go. "How long until the taxi's here?" I asked him.

He offered me a drink, maybe as a peace offering, but I ignored the drink that smelled like whiskey in his hand, and instead crossed my arms over my chest so that I could continue to glare at him. "The taxi, Rem. When will it be here?"

Rem shook his head, and I groaned. "I didn't call one. Thomas, come on. Just talk to me. So what if I said a word? People say it all the time. It doesn't mean anything."

Could he honestly be that fucking dense? Seriously? "Yeah, they do say it all the fucking time. But you don't. Or at least you didn't use to. And I never expected you to say it around me. I'm gay, or did that not cross your mind? Pretend to be straight all you want, but I'm gay, I'm out, I'm proud of who I am, and when you say crap like that, especially around me, it really fucking hurts. You wouldn't use racial slurs around the black members of your team, so why the hell would you use a word like that around me?"

I wiped at my eyes as hot angry tears fell down my cheeks. He looked hurt now, like maybe I was getting through to him. Which was great and all, but the point was he shouldn't have had to be told something like that. It was common sense and human decency to not act like an asshole around the people you cared about, or at all. I picked up my backpack and left the room. He had to move out of the way for me to get through the door, but that didn't seem to be a problem as he let me walk right by him.

"Where will you go?" he asked me.

"Hotel. I've already booked it." He sounded upset, but I didn't let that bother me. When he came up to rest his hand on my shoulder, I didn't move away, either. I'd told him not to touch me, and I hadn't just magically stopped being angry at him or forgiven him, but I had missed him over the past four years, and it was more than nice to be near him.

He pressed his lips to my shoulder, right above where his fingers were, and I lifted my hand to cover his. "I'm sorry," he said.

I nodded. I could tell that he was, but I didn't think that changed all that much. "I know. We'll try again another time."

"You sure you want to go?"

I looked over at him, at the unshed tears in his eyes, and the way he seemed to be silently begging me to stay, and I still nodded. I couldn't say the words because what wanted to come out was that of course I'd stay with him. I'd be stupid not to stay, I wanted to say.

But I had nodded because what he'd said wasn't okay, and I needed some space from him. "Okay. I'll go get you a cab."

I stood there in his expensive-looking living room with my hip against the couch we'd had sex on, and I desperately wanted to stay with him for the next few days instead of running away after only a few hours of being with him. When he came back with his phone still in his hand, I wanted to tell him that I'd made a mistake.

"The taxi will be here in ten minutes. Want to stay here and wait? You can. I'll leave you alone if you want."

He didn't come near me, didn't try to persuade me to stay, didn't do any of that. And I was grateful because if he had, I probably would have. I wasn't that strong around him. When he opened his arms to me, though, offering me a hug if I wanted it, I put my backpack down on the couch and went to him. It was good to be held, to feel his arms wrapping around me, and to feel like everything could be okay if he hadn't been an absolute moron.

"I'm sorry," he said with his forehead pressed against my neck.

I nodded. "I know you are."

A few minutes later the taxi driver called Rem to let him know he was there, and I grabbed my backpack.

"Will you call me when you get back to Colorado? Let me know that you got there okay?" he asked me.

I'd been pretty serious about not wanting to talk to him again, but I was also pretty sure we both knew that wouldn't last too long. I couldn't stay away from him if I'd tried. "I'll text you." He tried to hug me again as I was leaving, and I let him. And because it might have been the last time I'd get a chance to, I lifted my mouth to his and gave him a gentle kiss. He kissed me a little harder than I had kissed him, but I didn't pull away until he lowered his hand to my butt and gave me a hard squeeze through my jeans.

I stepped back and licked his taste from my lips as I shook my head. "We'll talk later."

He nodded and held the door for me as I left. The ride to the hotel was a miserable one, and I didn't say much more than the address I needed to go to because I was sure that the first words out of my mouth would have been me asking the driver to take me back to Rem's building. So I sat there in silence, then checked into my room, then lay there on the big king-size bed that I had all to myself.

CHAPTER THIRTEEN

"THIS FUCKING sucks," I grumbled to myself ten minutes after I'd arrived. I took out my phone, intent on playing a game, and instead called home. "Hey," I said to whoever picked up the phone.

"Thomas? Why do you sound so miserable?" Dad asked me.

So many reasons. So, so many. And none of them I wanted to talk to my dad about right then. He was a good guy and protective of his kids, so I knew there was no way in hell he was going to be understanding if he ever found out about why I was so mad at Rem right now. And since they had Madeline, I knew Rem was going to be in their lives, and therefore mine, for as long as he stayed interested in her because of his yearly phone calls.

"It's nothing, just the Oregon humidity getting to me I guess. Makes me all stuffy. Can I talk to Madeline?" I really needed to hear her voice. She was so young, so clueless, that I could talk to her and not risk giving away what a disaster this weekend had turned out to be.

"Sure, one second. I'll go get her from the living room. She's watching the penguins again. You must have really hated us when you got her that first movie. I swear…. Madeline, honey, Thomas wants to talk to you."

I was smiling as she answered the phone. I'd had no idea how the cute movie could make everyone but her miserable, but that was just about what it had done. "Hey, Thomas."

I put one of my arms behind my head, trying to get comfortable, and wished that Rem was there with me. I could have stayed, could have talked to him instead of just bolting. "Hey. Told you I'd call you."

"Yep. Penguins are funny when they dance."

"Because they wobble?" I asked her.

She giggled. "No! Because they've got big feet!" Her giggle turned into a laugh, and I closed my eyes. I should have stayed with Rem. I hadn't seen him in four years, so of course things were bound to change between us. He was going to change.

"Yes, they do. Hey, Madeline, I'm sorry, but I've got to go. I need to call someone. I'll talk to you tomorrow. Okay? Have a great night, don't eat too many cookies."

"How many is too many?"

I knew that question all too well. "How many have you had?"

"Three fingers."

She was four; she counted on her fingers. I thought it was plenty cute, so I didn't even correct her for saying *fingers* whenever she said a number. "One more. That's it."

"Mom! Dad!" She screeched into the phone. "Thomas said I could have one more cookie!"

I heard groaning in the background and shook my head. "No more after that one. Promise me?"

"Promise. Come home soon?"

I nodded. "Yeah, baby. I'll be home on Sunday night, and we'll hang out all of Monday. Sound good?" I'd taken Monday off too, because I'd be getting in late and had plans to take Madeline to the zoo.

"Yep. Bye?"

"Talk to you tomorrow."

"Okay. Bye." I heard her hand the phone off to someone, probably my Dad, who would have been standing nearby to make sure she didn't play with the buttons and accidently call random people again, and I hung up the phone. Should I call Rem? I didn't know. Did I want to call him? Yes, I did.

I chewed on my bottom lip as I hesitated with my fingers over the phone, though. I'd walked away from him less than an hour before. It was too soon. It was…. Oh screw it. I was calling him.

"Hi," he said on the second ring.

I licked my lips. "Hey."

"Thomas, I'm sorry."

"I know." I didn't need him to say it again. I knew he was. "It hurt that you'd say something like that in front of me. In Thornwood and even in Miami I never really got that kind of reaction from anyone. Everyone in my life has always been really accepting of me. That you said it…." I shook my head. "It hurt."

"I know it did. And I am sorry. Since you called does that mean you're speaking to me again?"

With a sigh I rubbed my free hand over my face. "I love you. I think trying not to talk to you would be worse than anything you could ever say to me. I just needed some time, some space to think."

"You had four years. And now you've had another hour. Can I see you again?"

I was ready to talk to him, but could I see him and not be angry with him? "Do you have a spare bedroom?" I asked him.

"Yeah. I do. Want me to come pick you up?"

"Please." I gave him the address. "I'll be ready to go when you get here. Just, Rem, don't be an asshole again this weekend. Please."

"I'll do my best."

That's all I could really ask of him. I started packing up the few things I'd taken out of my backpack while I heard him go down the elevator. "I talked to Madeline tonight." She was safe territory for us to talk about.

"She okay?"

"Yeah. I just promised her I'd call her every day that I was away." I zipped up my backpack and grabbed my room key. I'd reserved the room for the whole weekend, and I considered keeping it in case Rem did anything else to piss me off, but I knew I wouldn't go running away from him again. What he'd said had been stupid and callous and it had hurt a lot, but being away from him when we were finally in the same city again was even harder. I needed to be around him, to see him again. To touch him now that I finally could.

"This is the hotel you ran to?" He sounded fairly disgusted.

I laughed. "You're already here?"

"Yeah. Hurry?"

Whether he was afraid of someone eyeing his shiny black sedan in what wasn't even a rough part of town or if he was eager to see me again, I didn't know. And I guessed it didn't really matter all that much really.

"Leaving so soon?" the girl at the front desk asked me when I turned in my keycard.

I nodded to her. "Yes."

"Anything wrong with the room?"

"No. Just decided to go back and hang out at a friend's." She looked instantly relieved, as if me saying anything else would have landed her in trouble with her boss. "Thanks," I said when she handed me a receipt, which was thankfully only for the one night even though I'd booked the room until Sunday. I signed it, got my card back, and headed out to meet Rem.

"Hi," I said as I got into his car. It was dark in the sedan, but I was pretty sure he looked like he'd been crying too.

He gave me a little smile and pulled out onto the road. "Hey." He put his hand, palm up, in the center between us, offering it to me. I took it, holding the warmth of his fingers between my own. I loved him, and as mad as he'd made me, I wasn't going to avoid holding his hand.

We were back in his condo a few minutes later, and he showed me to his spare bedroom on the opposite side of the condo from his. It was well decorated, like the rest of the place, and not a single inch of it felt like the Rem I'd known in college.

"Where'd you get all this stuff?" I asked him as I put my backpack down and went over to an expensive looking white-and-blue vase that perfectly matched the shade of blue on the bedroom walls.

He shook his head. "I didn't. It came decorated like this when I bought the condo. I actually hate everything in it, but my parents insisted that I invest the money from my contract into something with substance."

It was the first time I could remember him mentioning his parents to me. I came out of the bedroom, and we headed over to the couch where we sat down together, and I put one leg up on it so I could face him better. "What are they like? Your parents?"

He gave me a weak little smile, but it dimmed quickly. "They're…. You know how some parents want their kids to be rich and others want them to be happy, and some think it's possible to do both?"

I shrugged. Maybe I did. Mine had only ever wanted me to be happy, so I guessed that it made sense that there would be other kinds of parents out there as well, ones I didn't agree with. But then again, they weren't my parents, so what did it matter to me?

"Well, mine are firmly in the stack of people that insist on money. It will make my life easier, it will get me a better wife, it will make everything I've ever wanted come to me…. Blah blah blah."

"And now you are rich, and you had a great wife," I told him.

"You thought Angela was great?" he asked me. He reached out to touch my hair, and I didn't pull away from him.

Nodding, I wondered why he looked so surprised. "I did. I hated sharing you with her, but I thought she was nice. I was mad at you for marrying her, though, because you didn't love her. And I thought you were just going to hurt her and that it made you a selfish prick. But I figured that maybe things would be okay, and you'd start to love her, and it would be good for you." I shrugged, because I'd thought they would have had the "Hollywood fairytale" kind of romance, and not the "divorced by the time he was twenty-four" kind of bittersweet ending.

He moved his hand to the side of my face, cupping my cheek with the warmth of his palm, and I leaned into his touch. It was so good to have him close to me again, and to not worry about him cheating with me anymore. "I missed you."

"I missed you too, Rem."

He leaned toward me a little, and I froze. "Can I kiss you, just one kiss?"

A kiss would be fine with me, as long as it stayed at only that. "I'd like a kiss, but I am still staying in the other room tonight. And I don't forgive you for what you did. I get why you did it, but you could have said anything else; you could have done anything else. You didn't have to say such a horrible word."

He nodded and helped pull me onto his lap so I was facing him. I was stiff as I sat down on his legs, and he ran his fingertips over my chest to finish their trail on the tops of my thighs where he squeezed me through the thick material of my jeans. "Rem...," I warned him.

He leaned forward to run his lips over the base of my throat. "I know. I said just one kiss. But tell me you aren't affected by me too, that you don't need me just as much as I need you right now."

Saying anything like that would have been a lie, so I simply folded my arms over his shoulders and kissed him.

"How do I make this up to you?" he asked me when I'd pulled away a few moments later.

I didn't know for sure, but I had things I wish I could've changed. "Are you still angry with Angela for not saying Madeline's name after a few years?"

He frowned up at me as he leaned his head back against the couch. "Yes. Why?"

"Call her, and find out why she did."

He looked like he would much rather have been doing anything else. "What will that change?"

I had no idea. "Probably nothing. But try it anyway." I slid off his lap so that he could call her. Did I want the man I loved calling the woman he was in the middle of getting a divorce from to talk about the daughter they gave up who I was now helping to raise? So very much no, I didn't. But if I was going to have a relationship with Rem, someday, then I didn't want this over us. I wanted a clear conscience, one that didn't include secrets and lies from my first semester in college.

I watched him from a giant fluffy chair, which was the only thing that really felt like Rem in the whole condo, and tried not to listen in on his phone call. "Hey, could we talk for a bit? … Now's good for me if it works for you. … Thomas is over here. … Yeah we do. Lots to talk about." He hung up the phone and looked over at me. "She'll be here in about half an hour."

Okay, I was not expecting that at all. "Huh? What's she doing in Oregon?"

He came over to sit with me, and since there wasn't enough room on the chair for both of us to sit together, I got up and sat down on his lap where he put his arms loosely around me. "We're keeping the divorce pretty quiet until it's finalized so she was here doing a Kraken spouse cooking special for a local morning news station. She got a two-week vacation with her friends out of it, so she wasn't too upset, but their Pacific Ocean cruise doesn't leave until tomorrow morning. You okay seeing her, or do you want to hide in the other room or something?"

I wasn't up to hiding, but I wanted to make sure I knew what was going on too. "How much do you want her to know?" I asked him.

"What are you okay with?"

Shrugging, I was pretty sure whatever he said, I'd be fine with her knowing. "You decide that. I never intended to get in the way of your relationship, and I'm not about to put myself into your divorce either."

He gave me a little smile and leaned forward to kiss my chin. "You didn't get in the way of her and me; that was my problem. I've never been all that good at being faithful. I know it's not the relationship that you want, but if you give us a chance, I'll do my absolute best to be only yours."

I'd thought, in all the years I'd known him, it had only been Angela I'd been sharing him with, and it sucked to be reminded that that hadn't been the case at all. "I'll need you to do more than try, Rem. If I'm yours, then you have to be mine. Nothing else. I don't want to compromise with you anymore. If I find out you've cheated on me then I'm gone."

He nodded and tightened his arms around my side, pulling me in closer to him. "I won't lose you again. Watching you walk away tonight… it was too much. I thought you were gone for good."

"I thought I was too. Turns out you aren't that easy to move on from." I turned my head so I could kiss his forehead, and I sighed. A comfortable silence stretched out between us as we waited for Angela to arrive. When there was a knock on the door, I got off his lap and headed into the kitchen. Baking cookies relaxed me, and if Rem had had anything to make some with, I would have done just that. But his kitchen was completely useless except for some soda, milk, and a decent selection of alcohol. I found enough that I could work with there and got to work making some drinks as she came in and I saw them hug.

"Hi, Thomas," she said to me as she came into the kitchen. She looked apprehensive, and like she didn't know what to do with me being there at the same time.

"Hey." I handed her a drink and hoped it worked to calm her down. "How've you been?" I sipped my own, and Rem came over to take one of the creamy alcoholic cocktails as well.

She gave me a shrug and looked over to Rem, then back to me, probably making her own assumptions about us. "Let's not play this game, Thomas. Please, not with you. I can't with you. Just... will you tell me the truth? I know Rem is useless with it."

"Hey!" Rem spoke up, sounding hurt.

I ignored him. "He wanted to talk to you, and I don't want to get in the way of that. But if you want to talk to me too, I'll be here. And if you want some privacy, I can go into the bedroom."

"Rem's?" she asked me pointedly.

I shook my head. "No. The blue one with the ugly vase thing."

Her expression brightened considerably. "It is pretty awful, isn't it?" I smiled at her. "How's...." She looked to Rem again, and the glass shook in her hands. "Is she happy?"

"You can talk to him about her, but you couldn't talk to me?" Rem asked her, coming around the island toward her.

Angela nodded shakily. "Yes." She put the glass down so that she could wipe at her eyes. "She was our little girl. Ours, Rem. Leaving the hospital without her...." She sniffled then turned her attention back to me. "She's happy, though, right?"

"Yeah. She is. Do you want to see pictures of her?" I offered.

She trembled and had to lean against the counter as she considered. "I haven't seen her since she was born. Not even a picture. Your mom… she offered, but I never could take her up on it. I think I'd like to see some pictures. I think I'm ready to see them. If you have any with you?"

I had hundreds, if not thousands, and they were all on my phone waiting for her. "Sure. Sit with me on the couch?"

Angela nodded, and the three of us headed over to the couch with me in the center, them on either side of me. I pulled my phone out of my pocket, swiped my finger across it to unlock it, and watched her smile as my background with Madeline eating cookie dough off a spoon popped up.

"Is that her?"

"Yes." I opened up my pictures and went to the folder that was just all about her. I hadn't let Rem scan through the pictures yet because he'd never asked, but now I handed my phone over to Angela and got up from the couch so they could sit together and look at all the pictures of Madeline I'd collected over the past four years.

I went to go sip my drink in the kitchen, close enough if they needed me for something or if my phone decided to act up like it sometimes did, but still far enough away I wouldn't be too much in the way if they wanted some privacy.

They talked quietly, but Angela couldn't be quiet as she cried, and I wasn't jealous when Rem put his arms around her and kissed her forehead.

"I'm sorry," he told her.

She nodded against his chest and continued to cry for a long time after that. After a while she seemed to have exhausted herself as she lay down on the couch and Rem let her rest as he came over to join me where I'd stayed in the kitchen.

"I had no idea that she missed her too. That she thought about her all the time. That it hurt her so much to give Madeline up," he whispered to me.

I hadn't known either, but then again I didn't talk to Angela at all. "Would you have stayed married to her if you had?" I asked him just as quietly.

He shook his head and stepped between my thighs where I was sitting on his counter. "No. I didn't love her, and we weren't happy. She deserves better than me. Thanks for telling me to call her. I'm glad Madeline has two people in this world who think about her all the time, even if she'll never really know either of us. Not like her parents anyway. I would like to meet her someday, though, if your mom says I can."

He rested his hands on the outside of my thighs, and I finished off my drink before I answered him. "I'll ask her when I get back on Sunday. She may not be ready for that, though—fair warning. She loves Madeline and only wants what's best for her. If she thinks that seeing you will confuse or upset her, then I don't think she'll say yes. It's in your agreement that you will see her when she's older and fully understands where she came from and who her family is, but I want you to know that it might not be right now."

Rem slowly nodded, though he did look disappointed by my words. And I wouldn't have blamed him one bit for feeling like that. Madeline was amazing and beautiful, and before I'd come to Oregon for the weekend, she was my one connection to Rem, my one way of being around him. She was the most precious thing in the world to me, and I wouldn't have risked her, either, so I knew where my mom would be coming from if she did say it was too soon for Rem to meet her. But I also wanted Rem to see Madeline and get to talk to her and see how wonderful she was for himself.

"Thomas?" Angela called to me, surprising me because my back had been to her, and I'd thought she'd still been asleep.

I turned to look over my shoulder at her and saw her watching us intently. I felt like she could see everything and knew everything, including how I'd been in love with her man for the last four years. It hurt to look at her for too long as the guilt built up inside of me. "Yes?"

"How long have you two been together?"

Her question was a simple one, but there was no easy answer to give her. Rem stepped back, putting a good three feet between us as if that made any difference in what we'd done. "Thomas, don't," he told me.

I sighed and looked up at him from my place on his island. "I get why you need to hide while we're out and why you can't come out. I do understand that. It's not how I am, but if you need it, then I think you're worth it. But if you want a real relationship with me, one where you can claim to be something more to me than just my friend and where I mean something more to you than someone to have sex with, then I need the people closest to us to know about us. And that includes Angela. You told me that you two have been friends for ten years. I know things happened, and I know we can't go back to how close the three of us were in college. I wouldn't want to. But as much as you'll let me tell her about us, I'd like to."

He pursed his lips and slowly shook his head. "And if I don't want her knowing anything?"

"She already can figure out some," Angela said coming up beside us. "Also, talking about someone when they're right there is rude. You boys should know that. Thomas, I expect the lies from Rem. I got used to them. The cheating wasn't the big surprise, since I kind of knew something was going on. But that he had this whole side of himself that he'd never shared with me broke my heart." She looked from me to Rem. "You were my best friend, and I loved you. There's no simple way to realize that the person you thought you'd grown up with never really existed. Help me figure out who you are now. I know we're getting a divorce. I won't try to stop that. All I want at the end of this is to know who you really are. Can you do that for me?"

Rem wiped at his eyes. "I'm so sorry, Angela. I never meant to hurt you."

"I'm sure you didn't," she said as she leaned against the counter not far from me. "So, Thomas, the truth. Please?"

I looked to Rem and waited for him to nod to me before I gave Angela the same. "Sure. As much as I know, I'll tell you."

She gave me a little smile and covered my hand with hers on the counter. "Were you with him when you knew he was with me?"

"Yes." She quickly pulled her hand back from mine, and I didn't try to bring her back to me. "When we first met, I didn't know he was with you." She didn't need those details, so I left them out. She didn't look that convinced, though, so I explained a little. "It was at a party."

"Right before the semester started. You couldn't come out," Rem filled in for her.

I didn't look at him. I couldn't. I'd been head-over-heels for him as a teenager. It had been my first time being in love. I was smarter now and liked to think I was more mature too, but that didn't mean one look back at him didn't send me right back to that place of seeing him sitting in that kitchen with a little smile on his lips and a purple mask covering up most of his face.

"So, you two have been having sex behind my back for the last few years, then?" She sounded like she hated us both, and I didn't blame her for that.

I waited for Rem to shake his head, to let her know that hadn't been the case, but he didn't. "If it's any consolation at all, which it probably isn't, once you were pregnant we stopped." As soon as the words were out of my mouth, I remembered the time in the woods by my house, and when I looked up, I found Rem looking back at me and knew he was thinking about that afternoon too. "Except for once," I clarified.

She slapped me, which I was expecting her to do. At least once or twice I'd wanted to slap Rem for being with other men since me. She was crying again as she slapped me across the same cheek. I deserved it, so I let her continue. If it made her feel better and less betrayed, then I'd let her hit me for the next hour. A third slap never came, though, and I lifted my gaze to find Rem's arms around her as he held her back. She struggled for a few seconds, then went limp in his arms.

"Don't leave angry," he told her when she started to storm over to her purse.

"You don't get to tell me what to do anymore!" She turned and screeched at him as she lifted a shaky hand in my direction. "It was bad enough that there were strange men that you were having sex with while you were married to me. But Thomas? He was my friend in college. He was your roommate. He's helping to raise our daughter. And you… you want me to be happy about this?"

I shook my head and decided to answer her before Rem could as she lowered her arm and wiped at her eyes. "No, Angela. I don't expect you to be happy. And if Rem does, then he's an idiot."

"Don't be a jerk," he snapped at me.

I lifted my eyebrows at him. "Think about things for a few minutes, and tell me that you weren't an idiot." While he was doing that, I got off the counter and went to Angela. "Hey. It's okay to hate me. It's okay to wish I was dead or that I'd never come into your lives."

She shook her head at me. "No, Thomas. I don't wish that. It's because of you that Madeline has a good home. I just wish that he hadn't been bi or hadn't been a cheating, lying, selfish bastard."

She was talking loudly enough for Rem to hear her, and I glanced back to see him rolling his eyes and making himself another drink, something hard and without any of the milk and soda I'd used before to cut it.

"Don't lose your heart to him," she told me as she reached out to gently touch me on the cheek that she'd slapped. It was warm, but I knew she hadn't hit me hard enough to really hurt me. "It's so easy to do, but it will hurt so much when he breaks it." I could have used her warning back in college. It might have actually made a difference then. But as I said good-bye to Angela at the door, I knew I wouldn't have been able to stop myself.

Rem was just impossible to ignore. And even a thousand miles away from him, I couldn't have stopped wanting him. I'd tried.

"So that was fun," he gruffly said to me after I'd finished locking the door up after Angela left.

I rolled my eyes at him. "It needed to be done. Honesty hurts."

"Not always," he countered. "Here's one that doesn't. I loved you in college. I was so scared to tell you, and Angela was in my life, but I did love you."

I smiled to him and dragged my fingers over the smooth marble counter he was sitting on. "I loved you back then too. Though I also thought you were an ass for cheating on your girlfriend."

He reached out and stopped my hand, pulling me to him. "Tell me you love me. You've never said it to my face."

I lifted myself up on my tiptoes so I could kiss him. "I love you, Rem. Sometimes I don't like you all that much or don't agree with you, but I've always loved you."

He smiled against my mouth and tangled my hands with his. "Well, that's something I guess."

I smirked and waited for him to say the words back to me. But he didn't, so I pulled away when he would have kept kissing me. "And?"

He gave me a sly little smile. "And?"

Rolling my eyes didn't help anything, but it did make me feel better. "Tell me you love me too. If you do."

He pressed a kiss to my forehead, then my temple, and finally my cheek. "I love you, Thomas. A lot. I'm sorry I didn't break things off with Angela when we got together. I'm sorry I can't be out with you and be everything that you want."

"Tell me you're sorry for having sex with other men while being in love with me and being married to her," I told him. I needed to hear it. I knew he loved me, had wanted me in those years we'd been apart, but it still really bothered me that he hadn't been faithful to her, if not to me.

His damn green eyes, that always seemed to be shining, were no less beautiful as he looked at me and gave me his softest and best smile. "I'm sorry that I let sex get in the way of us and ended up hurting two of the people I cared about most. I'm not sorry that you and I had sex or that I fell in love with you, but I am sorry that I was never honest with her or that I couldn't be faithful to you."

"Will you try harder?" I asked him. I didn't feel right asking him for absolute faithfulness, not when he lived in Oregon and I was in Colorado. But I wanted to know that while I was there and he was here, there weren't men in this place, that he didn't have guys on the side he didn't care about but still had sex with.

He nodded and put our joined hands between us on his thigh. "I will. I promise. I love you. I can't be out, but I do want to be yours, and I'll do whatever I need to do to make that happen."

"Thank you."

He gave me another kiss, and I pulled him to the couch with me where we spent the rest of the night cuddling and watching TV until we fell asleep together. It was just like old times, only better because now he could be only mine and our secret only had to be kept from strangers instead of those closest to us. It was still a compromise, but it was better, and it was one I felt like I could live with.

CHAPTER FOURTEEN

MONDAY MORNING I woke up in my own bed, and though I'd gone to sleep alone, I found the shape of a little girl tucked around my left arm. "Hey," I said sleepily. "Don't like your room anymore?" I asked her.

She woke up, and I brushed her blonde hair away from her face. She had Rem's loose curls, but her hair was just a few shades darker than Angela's. It was a good combination for her along with her eyes that were so much like Rem's. "Room's good. Was excited for the zoo."

I laughed and got out of bed to go shower and get dressed. "Zoo isn't until after breakfast. Go pick out your clothes. Shirt, bottoms, shoes. Skirt and leggings or jeans are okay. No jeans and a skirt this time." She gave me a little pout, and I laughed as I headed into the shower to get ready myself.

Coming back late last night, I hadn't intended to see Madeline until the next morning, but she and Mom were in my living room when I'd gotten in, waiting for me. No questions, thankfully, though I was sure they'd come later. But last night I just got the explanation that Madeline hadn't wanted to sleep in her own room since she'd wanted to see me so much. I could live with that.

When I got out of the bathroom, dressed in a soft T-shirt and a pair of shorts, Madeline was already waiting to get into the bath herself. She was pretty good about making sure the temperature was okay for herself, but I still helped her. And while she splashed bubble bath all over my bathroom floor where I could still see her in case she needed help, I went to make sure the clothes she'd picked out would be sort of okay for a day at the zoo. A purple shirt, a black tutu, and zebra print tights. I shook my head. At least she was going to be festive, and of course damn cute as well.

"All done!" she shouted at me a little while later as I'd been pouring cereal for us both.

I headed back in and helped her out, made sure she had her favorite big fluffy towel, then started to mop up some of the spilled water as she got dressed.

"Be ready to go soon," I called to her as I tossed the wet towels into the wash to run while we were gone.

"Tell me about Rem," she said as she came out of her bedroom. Her hair was a mess, but I kept a brush in the kitchen so I could brush her hair while she ate her cereal. It seemed to be the easiest compromise since she never seemed to sit still for me when I had her in front of the mirror.

"He's good, Cutie," I told her as she started to eat, and I began going through her tangles. "He says hi."

"What'd you do?"

A lot of things I would not be talking to her about. "Well… we ate seafood. And walked along a pier. And he showed me this really fancy restaurant."

"Did you like it?"

"Not really. They didn't have pizza." She made a sound like she was disgusted, and I laughed. "Maybe he'll come here someday." I'd been saying it idly, because I hoped he would, but we hadn't really made any plans for that.

"Would I get to meet him then?" she asked me.

I shrugged and stepped back from her hair. It was decent now. I wasn't amazing with hair, which was probably why mine was always so short, but at least her curls were untangled now. That was probably mostly due to the really expensive curl-detangler shampoo I bought for her. I was good with the cheap stuff, but it had killed her hair when she'd used it, so now I ordered her the good stuff.

"Maybe." I tried to never promise her anything I couldn't absolutely give her. "Would you like to?"

I sat down across from her and ate quickly. She was nearly done with her bowl and I didn't want her to have to wait on me when she was so looking forward to the zoo.

"I think so," she said, and that was that. I decided I'd talk to Mom about Rem meeting Madeline sometime soon.

It took over an hour to get to the zoo, and I'd forgotten that it was free day, so the zoo was packed. But with Madeline on my shoulders and my hands on her legs to keep her steady, she didn't miss a thing.

"Want to go into the reptile house?" I asked her. Normally she avoided it completely, even crying the one time I'd tried to show her that nothing in there could hurt her, but this time she laid her hands on my cheeks and made me nod. "Okay. We're going in." She laughed when I spun, nearly knocking over a trash can. We were still laughing together when we saw a giant Anaconda. I felt her shrink back a little, and she dug her hands into my hair, but I quickly moved on.

"Hey, baby, look at this thing. He's not so scary," I told her when we got to a glass cage that said it had a bearded dragon in it.

"I'd call him Spike," she declared. She wanted down, I figured as she squirmed on my shoulders, so I knelt to let her off. Surprising me, Madeline went right up to the glass and pressed her forehead against the bearded dragon's home.

"I have one of those," an older kid said, coming up beside her.

She turned to him. "You do not!"

"I do too!"

I pulled her back before they could get into a screaming fight about whether or not someone could buy a reptile in a store. The kid's dad came up and took him back too. "Sorry about that," he said.

I nodded and helped Madeline back onto my shoulders. "No problem. Does he really have one?"

The dad took his kid's hand. "Yeah. You can get them at most pet stores."

"I want one!" Madeline declared.

Great. "We'll look into it, baby."

"Spike! Spike! Spike!" she chanted all the rest of the afternoon at the zoo, and also while we were in the car, and then we were in a pet store where they did, in fact, have bearded dragons for sale.

"Do you know anything about them?" the salesman asked me.

I shook my head. "Not a clue. She saw one at the zoo, and now she thinks she wants one. They probably eat bunnies or something soft and cuddly like that right?"

The guy laughed. "No. Not at all. Here, I'll show you how we feed them." I held Madeline's hand as the guy, who couldn't have been more than a few years younger than me, pulled out a cup full of worms and began picking them up with his bare hands and tossing some into the Bearded Dragon cage. I was disgusted, Madeline gasped, and the dragons seemed ravenous.

"Here, you do it," he held the cup up to me, but I made Madeline go forward.

"Madeline, you want one of these guys, you're going to have to feed them. Try it." The brave little girl that she was, she scrunched up her face and did it, though she did squeal about it after she'd dropped a worm in for them.

I looked at the sales guy to see him smiling at me. "You're a good dad."

He had no idea who I was, clearly, but I liked the compliment. "Thanks." I could have explained to him how she wasn't my daughter, but that was a big story and one I didn't feel like telling him or thought he needed to know. "Are any of them calm enough for her to handle?"

He was quick to nod. "Sure. Of course." He took out a really big red one with a nearly black chin and held it out for Madeline to touch. Which of course she did, because I think she was half in love with the idea of having her first pet.

"Spike!" she cried out adoringly. She bopped him on his head, and I grabbed her hand back before he could bite her. But the bearded dragon just lay on the guy's hands, stretched out like he didn't care that a four-year-old had just hit him. "Can I hold him?"

The guy looked to me, I guess asking for permission, and I nodded. If Madeline thought she wanted to have a bearded dragon on her, then so be it. I thought she was going to cry to get it off her, but once the thing climbed up her chest and looked at me from her shoulder, she just started to run her hands down his big body. "Spike."

"We call him Ruby, because of his color," the guy said.

Madeline shook her head. "Spike." She looked up at me, with those big, pleading eyes I was pretty sure parents everywhere understood and had no defense against. At least I didn't. She could have asked me to invade another country to get her a pony and I probably would have if she kept looking at me like that. "Can I?"

"Are you going to help take care of him?" I asked her. I knew I'd be doing most of his care, but really, if she wanted a bearded dragon for a pet, then I wasn't going to say no to her.

She nodded, of course. I thought she might have promised anything right then. "Sure. We're getting a bearded dragon." I turned to look at the guy while she excitedly ran her hands over the dragon's back. "We'll need everything for it. Of course."

Everything for a bearded dragon turned out to be a few hundred dollars, but Madeline was damn happy, and my credit cards would recover just fine once I got a few paychecks in. I took a picture of her holding him and sent it to my mom and dad with the caption *She's bringing home a monster. Her first pet.* I decided to add Rem to the list of recipients and sent it off.

On the way home, I got to check my messages at a stop light, while also keeping an eye on Madeline to make sure she didn't take Spike out of the cardboard box he'd been put into. My mom didn't want it in her house. Dad said I was a pushover for getting it for her. Rem, though, he surprised me with his message of *Nice. A bearded dragon. Great first pet choice.*

Once we were home and I had the dragon set up, if Madeline ever let it go into its massive new cage, I called him. "Hey."

"Hey. Nice picture."

I sat down on the couch and watched her playing with her new pet in the middle of the room. Spike apparently needed to come to a tea party where bugs would be served just for him. I shook my head. "How'd you know what it was?"

"I'm allergic to dogs, cats, guinea pigs, ferrets, horses, rabbits, rats, mice… pretty much if it's fluffy and most people would consider it a pet, I can't be around it without getting hives. So I had a bearded dragon growing up."

I was smiling as I lay back on the couch. "I never told you that Madeline was allergic to dogs too, did I?"

"She is?"

Nodding, I looked over at her. She looked ecstatic about her new pet. "They make her sneeze. She doesn't get hives, thankfully, but yeah, she's allergic. I don't know about cats, though."

"Poor kid."

"It's not so bad. Now she has a pet called Spike, and that is going to be so cool once she starts school in a couple of years. How are you anyway? I miss you." Less than twenty-four hours away from him and I was already wishing I could get on a plane and go back there to see him.

"I miss you too. Wish we'd had more time together. And that you had slept in my bed more."

I smiled. I'd only spent the one night in his bed, and I regretted that a bit since I shouldn't have ever left his bed. "Don't make me mad next time."

"I won't. As long as you promise not to make it be four years before I can see you again."

I was absolutely sure it would not be that long. "I'll make sure I see you before then."

"We play the Colorado Blizzards in a few months. If your parents were okay with it, I'd like to sneak up to see you both that day. I could get you tickets to the game too."

"The Colorado whoseits?" I asked him, completely confused.

He laughed, and I smiled. "Your football team. Don't you follow football?"

"I follow you," I corrected him. "I'd follow you in those white pants all day."

"Ha-ha. Ask your parents. I gotta go get to practice. Be good."

"I will. Bye, Rem."

"Bye, Rem!" Madeline yelled over to me.

"Did you hear her?" I asked him.

"Yeah. I did. Say hi to her for me. Bye. I miss you. I love you."

It was so good to hear those words from him, especially now he'd said them to my face. "I miss you and love you too. Go try not to get hurt before the season even starts. I need you here in a few months."

My parents agreed, thankfully, but my mom still wasn't entirely convinced Rem wouldn't try to take Madeline at some point. I knew she was scared, and I wished I could help ease her worries. I guessed only time around him would make her realize he wasn't going to be a threat to us.

It was a cool November morning with snow just starting to trickle down, when Rem pulled up in front of my townhouse. I'd been watching for him out the front window with my feet tucked up under me and a mug of hot chocolate in my hands. Madeline sat on the floor with Spike, trying to get him to eat some kale out of her hand. Mom and Dad, and probably Dusty too, would be over later, but for the first time of Rem seeing Madeline, I wanted it to just be us. I got off the couch as he came out of his rental car.

"I'm going to go outside for one second. Be good," I told Madeline. "And don't drink out of my hot chocolate."

She pouted but waved happily to me anyway as I went out front.

Rem wrapped me in a hug, and I held on to him for a few seconds longer than was strictly necessary for a hug between friends, but for a lover I hadn't seen in three months, it wasn't nearly enough.

"Hey," I said, stepping out of the hug but still keeping my hand on his stomach.

He grinned at me. "Hey yourself. God I missed you." I wanted to kiss him but knew he'd likely pull away. A hug was one thing. A kiss wasn't nearly as easy to explain if anyone happened to be watching us. This was Thornwood, the quietest little town I could imagine, but with Rem being on TV and all, I didn't want my needs to be the reason his career had an issue.

"I missed you too. Three months without you sucked."

He tried to push me toward the door. "Then let's go inside, and we can make it up to each other. I don't have long before I have to meet up with the team for practice."

I knew that, and I wanted him all to myself. But there was someone he needed to say hello to before I could enjoy my time with him. "First, I want you to meet someone. Again."

His eyes got really wide, and I smiled up at him. "She's here?"

I nodded. "Right inside. You ready? If you're not I'll text my mom, and she'll come get her, and we can go to the diner for breakfast or something. But if you want to meet her, I'm sure she'd like to say hi to you too. She talks about how you both have bearded dragons all the time. She doesn't understand that you had yours when you were a kid. She just thinks it's more funny that you have one too."

"She does?" He looked past me to the door.

"Yes. Ready?" I asked him. He gave me a little nod, like he wasn't completely sure of himself, but I opened the door anyway. "Hey, Cutie, I brought someone here to see you," I told her.

She looked over at us from where she was holding Spike on her lap and gave Rem the biggest grin I'd ever seen her give anyone. "Rem!" she squealed, before dumping a disgruntled Spike onto the carpet and charging over to him. I didn't get a hug or anything, but he did as she ran into his arms and he lifted her up. I saw the unshed tears in his eyes and patted his shoulder as I walked past him to go put Spike back into his cage. The damn thing took up a good third of my living room, but whatever. He made Madeline happy.

"I saw you on TV last night," Madeline said to Rem.

"Really? What was I doing?" He sounded so fucking happy. I was really glad for him as I turned back to see him sitting down with her on the couch.

"Tossing a football. Can you show me how? Thomas is horrible at sports."

Rem laughed, and I snorted. I could have denied it, but really what was the use? She was right. I could hardly throw a football farther than she could. "Yeah, I can show you."

"Anyone want some hot chocolate?" I asked as I went into the kitchen.

"Me!" Madeline said, raising both of her arms in the air to get my attention. Of course she did; the girl never got enough sweets.

"Rem?" I asked him as I started hers.

He gave me a nod, and I saw him smile. "Yes, please."

I started one for him too. "Two hot chocolates coming up. Now, it's early, but Madeline and I did make some cookies last night. Do you want one, Rem?"

"Have one. Please?" Madeline begged him.

I knew he was done for before he even laughed. "Sure. A cookie too."

"Me too!"

Yep, I'd figured that. "Wash your hands before cookies since you were handling Spike."

I knew she would, though it might take another reminder to get her to do it. I washed mine quickly too while I waited for the milk to get warm on the stove. They got up from the couch, and Madeline showed Rem her pet. I couldn't wait until she was in kindergarten next year and could take him to class for show-and-tell. Some of the kids would be terrified, I was sure, but she handled him like a pro, as long as she wasn't dumping him on the floor. And I hadn't been too excited about him at first, but I had to admit he'd grown on me as a decent sort of pet. He didn't bark or make her have an allergic reaction or care when I had to work a double at the grocery store because someone couldn't bother to come in.

We sat down for cookies and hot chocolate on my couch with Rem next to me and Madeline on my lap since Rem took up most of the couch. He was all muscle, I knew, and he'd filled out a lot since college. But he was still so much taller than I was. I only really noticed it, though, when I was trying to kiss him and he hadn't yet bent down to kiss me back.

"You really made these? They're great," Rem said when he'd finished off his fourth.

Madeline nodded. "I have a company."

He looked from her to me, and I nodded. "It's still going. Though we did cut back on custom orders. We only do those around the holidays now."

"Nice." He moved his hand toward me, and I took his fingers in mine. "Must be fun."

I smiled at him and laid my head on his shoulder. He didn't have much longer with me, I knew, and I didn't want him to go. "It is."

"At the game tonight, when you come in, give any of the people checking tickets your name. You'll be taken to the box, and I got enough passes for your parents too, if they want to come," Rem told me softly as Madeline got off my lap and went to go stare at Spike through his cage for a while.

I nodded. It would be good to see him play for the first time in person now that he was a big shot professional. "Are you nervous?"

He chuckled and turned his head to kiss my forehead. "No. I'm a first-string tight end, but it's not like I have the kind of responsibility that comes with being the quarterback."

"Do you like this position better or do you wish that you were still a quarterback?" I asked him without raising my head from his shoulder.

He lifted his hand to my cheek and turned my face so he could kiss me. I curled my fingers in the front of his shirt. If Madeline had been with my parents right then, I would have been pulling him into my bedroom for as much fun as we could manage before he had to go. But I was glad he'd been able to meet her, even if it did mean I had to share him.

"It's going to be hard to go back to Oregon and know that I can only see her once in a while," Rem whispered far too quietly for Madeline to hear him.

I nodded. I was sure it would be, now he'd met her. "Once my parents say it's okay, I'll bring her with me whenever I come for a visit if you want."

He gave me a little smile, then looked back over at her. "What if I got a place here? In Thornwood? Or somewhere close enough to here? I couldn't stay here all year, but during the off-season we'd have a few months together before training started up again."

Was he being serious? Of course I wanted to see him all the time. "Yes. Please."

He kissed me again, and I clung to him as tightly as I could until he had to leave again. Madeline hugged him good-bye and I kissed him, and even though I'd see him from a distance in a few hours, it wasn't nearly the same.

"Will you have any time tonight before you leave again?" I asked him as we stood on the front porch with Madeline in my arms and the snow falling heavier around us.

"Maybe. It will be late, though, and I'd have to leave early."

A few hours with him would be better than nothing, I knew. And I was desperate to get as much time with him as possible. I put Madeline down so I could take my extra house key off the ring. I didn't even think twice about handing it to him. "Use it whenever you're in town. You're welcome here."

He smiled at me and gave me a big hug. "Thank you," he whispered in my ear.

"See you tonight," I whispered back to him.

When he pulled away, he was grinning at me as he pocketed the key. "Yeah, you will."

The promise in his words made me blush, and Madeline and I waved to him as he drove off, back to Denver. We had a few hours to kill before we had to head down for the game, so I took her over to my parents' house.

The game was pretty boring actually. Me not being a football fan and having a kid next to me who was easily distracted, I spent most of the time that I wasn't watching Rem on eating or trying to entertain Madeline. The box seats were nice, complete with massages if I wanted them and a free buffet, but I would have rather been down on the first row where I didn't have to squint to see Rem running around on the field.

At halftime I'd had enough, and I took Madeline, and we headed down the long line of steps and through a lot of people wearing Blizzard light blue, down to the first row of seats. They were full, and I likely couldn't have afforded their purchase price anyway, but it was nice to stand by the railing and look at Rem as he drank some water and ran a towel over his face. I wasn't going to say anything to him or even try to get his attention, but Madeline had other ideas apparently as she crouched down, put her arms through the metal bars, and started shouting for him. "Rem! Rem! Over here! Rem!" she shouted until he turned in our direction and smiled at us.

People were starting to notice us, but even more turned to look as Rem walked over to us and gave her a high five through the bars. "Hey. What do you think of the game?" he asked her.

"Food's good."

I snickered. That was about what I thought of it too. If I thought Rem was going to be upset by our apparent lack of interest in his career, I would have been wrong. He just laughed and reached his hand through the bars to touch my ankle. I crouched down beside Madeline to be able to see him better. "Can't we just come down there and sit next to you on the field? I'll get you water. Or a towel. Or something," I practically whined at him.

He blushed, and I was glad he'd been thinking along the same lines as me. "Can't. I'd get in trouble."

"Daniels!" one of the coaches, I had no idea which one, called to him.

"Gotta go." He gave my ankle another squeeze before taking off again, and I stood there with Madeline until someone official looking told me I had to go back to my seat. With a sigh I picked Madeline back up, and we made our trek to the box area again. The buffet had been changed out, and I grabbed some sushi and some chips for Madeline before we took our seats.

"How long have you been with the team?" the woman beside me asked as I got comfortable.

"With the team? I'm not." I ate a piece of sushi and shrugged. It was pretty good, especially since we were in Colorado.

She smiled at me. "No. That's what we say. Those of us who have husbands or boyfriends on the field."

"Oh." I blushed. "I don't. I'm just friends with one of the players. From college." I hoped that sounded fairly normal and boring.

"Ah."

Well that could have meant anything, and I wasn't interested in trying to figure it out. Some people she knew came in, and she started talking to them, which meant I got to be left alone and out of her line of questioning.

"I'm bored," Madeline complained at the start of the fourth quarter.

"Me too." I'd tried to pretend to be otherwise for hours, and my patience was growing pretty thin. At least the Kraken were winning. I knew enough about football to know what their score meant. Madeline had a hard time sitting still during most things. Movies in a theater were typically out of the question, so I wasn't all that surprised when she'd had enough ten minutes before the end of the game.

"Well, you hung on for a long time," I told her as I scooped her up and we started heading back down to the railing where we could watch Rem for the last few minutes. I was really glad I had too, because that meant I got to see him make his first pro touchdown. I'd seen him do it plenty of times in college, but a pro touchdown was a much bigger deal. And Madeline and I were right there to cheer him on as the Blizzard fans around us booed.

"Why do they do that?" Madeline asked me while they were still booing and the Krakens won.

"Because they're idiots."

She giggled and tightly wrapped her arms around my neck. I was hoping we'd get another few minutes with Rem now the game was over, but they were all ushered off the field. I headed home with a little girl who was happy Rem had won but also that we no longer had to sit around waiting for something to happen too.

When we got back to Thornwood, I left Madeline with my parents, because I was expecting Rem to come visit me, and I headed home to relax for a while.

CHAPTER FIFTEEN

I HAD tried to stay awake for Rem. I really had, but it didn't work. I didn't know what time I'd finally fallen asleep, but it must have been after eleven because the news was the last thing I remembered watching before I felt Rem climb in bed with me.

"Hey," he said as he wrapped his arm around my chest and pulled me back against him. "Is Madeline with your mom and dad?"

I nodded and rubbed myself against him. "Yeah. How long can you stay?" I turned over in his arms, and he moved between my legs. I'd gone to bed naked, and he was quick to run his hands over my hips and inner thighs before cupping me.

"Only until four. We've got three and a half hours before I need to get back to the team."

Well that really sucked. "Should we just cuddle and rest, then?"

Laughing against my lips, he rubbed his cock against mine before kissing me. "Fuck no. I want you. I brought you both jerseys. Wear it and miss me."

I nodded against his lips and sighed as he started to get me ready for him. "God I miss having you under me when you're gone," he said.

I arched as he slid inside of me. I could have used more time, more lube, but I wasn't about to ask him to stop now that he was in. It was so much better just to adjust while he thrust into me, and I rode him out. I slipped my legs around his waist and clung to him.

"You're still just as tight as you were in college," he mumbled against my lips as he slammed me into the bed. It creaked under us each time either of us moved, and I knew I'd need to get a new, much better bed if he was going to be around more often. Either that or keep Madeline at my parents' when he was over.

"Four years of abstinence," I reminded him. He kissed the side of my throat, sucking on me, and I closed my eyes and just held on to him. "I need this more," I said between gasps.

"Me too."

Coming with him in me was always a great experience, and that night was no different. He finished in me, and maybe I should have cared that he hadn't used a condom that time, but I didn't. We lay together, with his arm over my stomach, and I wished that we could have stayed that way for a lot longer than the few hours that I had left with him.

TWO MONTHS later the season was over, and I was back in Oregon, back in his condo, and back in his arms. "I'm sorry Madeline couldn't come," I told him as I sat on his lap.

He nodded and kissed the base of my throat. "I know. I talked to your mom. She's not ready yet, but she said soon. She wants me to get that condo that's for sale a few doors down from you. Said it would be a good step if I wanted to be a part of Madeline's life."

It didn't surprise me that he and my mom talked. They'd started doing it more and more since he'd met Madeline. I frowned and pulled back at the mention of the condo, though. "What one that's for sale? None of them are for sale that I know of."

He frowned right back at me. "The cop's one? Your cousin?"

Oh. Trent. "Yeah, he's not really my cousin. Our moms worked together a long time ago. He's moving out of Thornwood? Is that what she said?" Trent had always lived in Thornwood, same as me. Our moms had been best friends and even given us names that started with the same letter, even though we were a lot of years apart. I didn't know how the decision was made, but I liked my name more than his, as long as no one tried to shorten it. I wasn't a Tom, Tommy, or Tommie, like some people had tried before.

"Your mom didn't go into all the specifics, just that he was moving in with his boyfriend at some point, and the condo would become available."

"You probably should have led with that. Makes much more sense now," I said, grinning at him. "You know the townhome with the cop sign on the door?" He probably didn't. Every house on the row looked exactly the same.

He shrugged. "Maybe? As long as I knew which one was yours, usually by the bright chalk drawings on the sidewalk, I honestly didn't pay much attention to any of the rest of it."

"Makes sense. Not like you need to know who everyone in the row is. Are you considering it?" I'd love to have him so close. I wasn't ready to live with him, and my townhouse really wasn't big enough for both of us, but having him a few doors down from me would be really nice. "We could see each other all the time in the off-season. We could go to the zoo and museums and puppet theater events."

He laughed and leaned forward to kiss my neck. I shivered as he ran his chapped lips over my skin. "Those sound great. But how about something for just us?"

I leaned into his touch and sighed as he dragged his fingertips down my chest. I had on way too many clothes for this conversation. "Well, I've got a bed…," I offered, making him laugh.

He lifted me up, because he was just that fucking strong of course, and laid me down on the couch on my back. "I have a bed too. You might remember it, though I think you need to spend more time in there this trip."

He was right. I never wanted to leave it. "Are you really considering spending part of the year in Thornwood and part here?" I asked him as I started on the buttons for his button-down. I understood that he'd probably wanted to look nice while picking me up from the airport, but seriously—T-shirts and loose shorts were so much easier to get off. He needed to get with the program. If I couldn't have him naked all the time, then at least I needed to be able to get him that way as quickly as possible. Once I had his shirt off, I went for his pants.

Where he was wearing a belt. "Before you answer that, you and I need to talk about how to dress when you pick me up. Your clothes need to be easy to get off."

He smiled at me and dipped his hips into my hand, letting me get a good feel of his hard cock waiting for me. "What if I want to take you to a nice restaurant before I come back here and screw you?"

I snorted and shook my head. "I like pizza. I like takeout. The fanciest I get when I'm not with you is making actual chicken that doesn't already come precooked and breaded in little shapes. All of the food in my kitchen is kid-friendly and can be made into a meal in less than fifteen minutes."

He looked surprised, and I shrugged. "Most of the time I'm cooking with a kid around," I reminded him.

"I'm insanely jealous of you," he said before giving me a rough kiss. "And yes, I am thinking about moving there. Your mom gave me Trent's number. I'm planning to call him tomorrow."

"That's…. Wow." Not eloquent, but I was pretty freaking happy I could be getting him all the time during the off-season. It wasn't like it would be full time or anything like that. But for a few months out of the year, it would be like he was mine.

He nodded and kissed my chin. "Would that be okay with you? Last time we lived that close was college. Five years ago."

"Yes." I was very sure I'd be okay with him living just a few doors down from me. I got his pants open, despite his damn belt, and slipped my hand inside his boxers to stroke him.

Rem rested his forehead on the couch cushion beside me as I ran my hand over his hard cock and smiled up at the ceiling. I loved being able to have that effect on him where I could reduce him to mutters and sharp gasps against my neck.

"I was going to talk to you about more than that," he said as he thrust into my hand.

"Like what?"

He licked up the side of my neck, and I gasped. "If I came out, would you still love me?"

I thought that was a pretty stupid question for him to ask me. Because of course I would love him. I was pretty sure I would always love him. "Yes."

"There would be controversy," Rem warned me, as if I already didn't know it would come to that. There were no out football players, at least not current ones.

Whatever happened, though, I knew I could handle it. I wasn't so sure about him, since it could mean the end of his career in professional football, but if he thought he might want to come out sometime, I certainly wasn't going to tell him not to. "As long as it doesn't affect Madeline, I'll be fine. And I know you're strong enough to handle it."

He frowned down at me and didn't look nearly as sure of himself as I was. "And if I'm cut from the team?"

I could hear the fear, the worry in Rem's voice, and I lifted my mouth to be able to kiss his chin. I couldn't reach much more than that without him bending down to meet me. "You don't have to come out. I understand how important it is for you to play football, and I wouldn't want you to jeopardize that. I'm okay like this. It's not ideal, but it is working right now."

"If I'm not out, though, I can't marry you," Rem quietly told me.

My breath caught sharply in my chest, and I stared up into his gaze and those impossibly gorgeous green eyes of his. I thought he'd be joking or try to laugh it off at least. But he didn't. Instead he cupped my face with his hand and leaned down for a kiss. "Yes," I whispered, still licking his taste from my lips when he'd pulled back.

"Yes, what?"

I smiled against his mouth. He knew damn well what. "Yes, when you're ready to ask me to marry you, I'll say yes to you."

"I could be a penniless ex-football player with a washed-up career and too much controversy to be touched by any sponsors," he warned.

It was funny, actually, how much he seemed to think that would bother me. "My answer is still yes." He kissed me hard enough to take my breath away, and I wrapped my arms around his shoulders. What he didn't understand was that my answer would have always been yes. I'd loved him in college, and my feelings for him had only grown over the years I didn't have him.

"You're too good to me," he whispered against my lips. "All the crap I put you through." He shook his head, and I gave him a hard squeeze, not hard enough to hurt him, but enough to shut him up for a minute and let me talk.

"We're good for each other," I corrected him. Yeah, he'd put me through some things he shouldn't have. But I'd forgiven him for it, and I was ready to move on. He kissed me again, and I helped him get the rest of his clothes off. For me getting naked meant pushing off shorts that had an elastic waist and stripping off a T-shirt. My flip-flops were already off.

I groaned as he entered me a few minutes later, and I wrapped my arms around him. My favorite part of sex with Rem was how we held each other, like there couldn't ever be space between us, and he was just as desperate to keep me close as I was with him.

Sated and happy much later, I lay naked beside him on the couch as he ran his fingertips down my side. "I love you. If I don't tell you that enough, I do love you. I need you to know that," he murmured against my ear.

I smiled and tried very hard not to laugh as his stubble tickled my earlobe. "I love you too."

"Good. Then you'll forgive me for the TV interview I have to do tomorrow."

Groaning, I wanted to glare at him, but I was too comfortable being held by him with his muscular arms wrapped tightly around me. "You said we'd have the week together. Just the two of us. No work," I reminded him.

He kissed my temple, then my cheek. "Just this one. It'll be a good one. Talking about my first winning season. All the rookies are getting interviews this week, according to my agent. I might even get a toothpaste advertising deal soon."

I snorted. "What don't people want you to endorse at this point?" Toothpaste, tortilla chips, pizza… I was kind of glad I didn't live in Oregon because I saw some of the really awful commercials he was in, and I thought it would be hard not to laugh at them when he was around if I saw them all the time. It wasn't that he was bad in them, but they were pretty bad and I cracked up. So did Madeline, so maybe that didn't make me such a bad person for finding them as funny as I did.

"Wedding rings, seeing as how I'm divorced and all," Rem answered me seriously after a few minutes. I hadn't realized he was actually thinking about my question about the endorsements. I had been joking, not expecting a real answer from him.

I nodded. "Angela okay? Have you talked to her since it was finalized?"

He gave me a squeeze. "It's really sweet that you actually ask about her, instead of being damn glad she's gone so I'm all yours. But yeah, she's good. Still in Miami. Dating this guy that's a friend of her dad's and also a senator. Maybe she'll make a political run for something or other someday. I wished her luck, and she said to say hi to you for her."

"Huh. That's nice of her," I said.

"Yeah. It's good that she forgave you for having sex with me. She's still a long way from getting over what I did to her, but I understand that, and I'm okay with it. I shouldn't have married her or stayed with her for as long as I did. But I met you because she wanted to go to Miami College, and Madeline is in this world because of her, so I'm going to be grateful to her for the rest of my life for those things."

I smiled and ran my hand over his arm that crossed my chest. It was good to hear him talking like that and actually acknowledging everything he'd done wrong in his relationship with her. But there were good parts too, and Madeline was a huge part of that. I turned over in his arms, but I nearly fell off the couch, and would have, too, if he hadn't caught me before I fell.

"To the bed?" he asked me.

"Shower first?" I was pretty sticky, actually.

He gave me a grin, and I got up, already knowing where his mind was going and not minding the direction at all as he followed me into the shower and his mouth found mine under the hot spray.

THE NEXT afternoon I sat on his couch, watching the TV with an extra-large pizza with everything but anchovies laid out in front of me. If I was going to be alone in his condo and watching his interview, I figured that at least I was going to be comfortable doing it. He didn't have any beer, but he did have enough alcohol in the house that I could make a few different things. I started with whiskey on the rocks, with three ice cubes because I couldn't handle it without it being watered down at least a little bit, and turned the channel off the action movie I'd been watching to the channel he'd told me to have it on.

He was already on the screen, sitting there across from a man I recognized instantly. "Fuck," I swore, wondering if the guy that had asked him if he was gay months ago had always been a reporter, or if he'd been a fan and a reporter… I shook my head. "Please don't ask him if he's gay again," I told the TV, even though I knew Andy couldn't hear me through it. "Please be good, Rem." I really didn't want to be mad at him so soon. Not when it was so much more fun just to enjoy getting to spend time with him.

"Hello, Mister Daniels. We actually met a few months back, at Darcia's restaurant downtown. How've you been?" Andy began the interview by asking him.

It was almost comical to watch the recognition come over Rem's face. If I didn't love him, I would have laughed. Since I did care about him, though, I ate my pizza, sipped the whiskey, and hoped nothing bad came out of the live interview.

"There you go. Yep, this is that guy," I told the screen when it was clear Rem remembered everything. Yeah, he'd said he wasn't a fag to this guy. And I'd walked out of his condo. I'd been pissed at him that night, and remembering made me mad at him too, but not nearly as much. And I still thought it was one of his stupider moments.

Rem's smile was totally fake, and it made me laugh. His first TV interview, as far as I knew, and he looked terrified already. "Hi, Andy. I do remember you. How've you been?"

Andy's friendly expression was much more genuine, and I wished Rem would relax a little and become more comfortable. Maybe if he took off his shirt. Actually that wasn't a bad idea. I took another slice of pizza and thought about how much better the interview would be if he didn't have a shirt on and everyone else watching got to see those lovely muscles. I licked my lips just thinking about his abs. He'd been fit in college, but now he was built, and he was all mine. I grinned thinking about his abs under my fingertips, that little trail of nearly black hair that ran from his navel to his cock. "I've been good. Really good. But maybe not as much as you. That touchdown you had at the end of last season against the Demons, that was something special. Have you had many game-winning touchdowns like that in your career?"

Boring, boring... I wanted his shirt off. I'd promised Rem that I would watch the interview because it was important to him, but I figured that didn't mean I couldn't do other things at the same time. I took out my phone and brought up this new jousting game I'd just found the day before.

"I haven't, and that, along with a championship, seems to be the two biggest goals for people in this career. That I got one of those goals in my rookie season was huge for me."

"Good answer, Rem," I said, looking up at the screen. He seemed to be a little more relaxed now, his smile looking less forced and a bit more genuine. Now if he could only look a little less scared, this could turn out to be a good interview for him as far as I was concerned. Hopefully no one else noticed how ridiculously uncomfortable he looked talking about himself like he was.

"Were you at all disappointed that you didn't make it beyond the regular season?" Andy asked him.

"Well, of course he was. They don't play not to win." That was a little bitchy, sure. But really what did Andy think his answer was going to be? That it didn't matter and he didn't care? Uh, nope.

"I was disappointed," Rem began. "I'm competitive, and I like to win. But I realize that there are other years to win and get a ring. This year wasn't the one for the Kraken. Hopefully next year will be better. I plan to be in this game for a long time, and I hope to continue on with the Kraken. I've been incredibly lucky so far in my career. I look forward to many more years with them."

For being his first live interview, I thought Rem was doing a pretty good job. Not bad at all, actually. Much better than I would have been, but then again I was horrible at talking to strangers, and the cameras would have probably made me pretty miserable. "What, to you, are the biggest differences between college football and where you are now as a professional?" Andy asked him.

I snorted. That was easy—the money. I got up to get a soda since my whiskey was gone. I didn't give myself all that much to start with, so it wasn't as if I'd downed half the bottle or anything. And, it looked like Rem wasn't much of a drinker either, since most of the same bottles that had been there last time were there still, and they weren't much emptier than they had been when I'd poured drinks for Angela, Rem, and me.

"The guys I'm with now, they're a lot more dedicated than the ones I knew in college," I caught Rem saying as I came out of his kitchen. "It's good to be surrounded by so many serious people who can really concentrate now that I'm in the pros. I'm in good company with my team, and I appreciate the guys for everything I've learned already."

Andy smiled and I liked how happy Rem had started looking. Maybe being interviewed on live TV was going to be just another thing he was really good at. "Now for a far more… personal question, Mr. Daniels."

"Go for it," Rem said easily. I wondered if there was really anything else he could have said at that point. No? I don't want to answer any personal questions? Nope, he had to agree, I felt.

"After your divorce from your wife, Angela Bakerton, we haven't really seen you with any female friends while you've been out."

"Oh shit." I leaned toward the TV, wondering what the hell Andy was up to. "Rem, don't say the f-word. Don't say it. Nope. If he asks you if you're gay, find a better way to say that you aren't. Don't drop the word on live television." I realized I was begging the TV, but whatever.

Rem didn't say anything as Andy continued. "And that has led to some interesting rumors that you might be bisexual or gay. What do you have to say to fans who might be wondering about that very question right now?"

I shook my head in disgust. "That you're a fucking nosey asshole," I grumbled.

But Rem just smiled. "Well, Andy, I can confirm that those rumors are true. I am bisexual, and I am currently in a relationship with someone special who I have known for a long time now."

Exclusive Excerpt

Somewhere to Belong

A Thornwood Novel

By Caitlin Ricci

Needy. Obsessive. Clingy. Twenty-five-year-old Eli Walker has heard it all. That's why he doesn't bother calling back the guys he's been with anymore. Sex should be about fun, not a relationship, and no one has complained about him getting overly attached in years. If only he actually felt wanted for once instead of empty and used when guys are done with him.

Grayson Pendleton is a wealthy business consultant with clients all over the world. His life is often glamorous, but it leaves him no time for a relationship, and at forty-eight, he's starting to notice the lack of romance in his life. His only romantic connection is Eli, but they're just two guys who have sex occasionally. It took him months to get Eli's first name, and even now they only communicate through a hookup app.

When Grayson inherits a house in Thornwood, Colorado, it's one more thing he doesn't need in his life, and he knows he won't be there enough to enjoy it. Still, the old house has the potential to be a home, and more importantly, it gives Grayson a chance to save Eli when he needs it most.

Coming Soon to
www.dreamspinnerpress.com

CHAPTER ONE

Eli

HOTEL ROOM 221 was held slightly open with a doorstop, just as PendletonGray had promised it would be. The lights were on, and I smiled as I leaned against the door to close it behind me. It locked on its own, and I quickly stripped off my T-shirt and tossed it onto a nearby chair. PG, as I'd taken to thinking of him over the past two months since we'd first started hooking up, lay stretched out on the bed with a sheet over his lap. It was bunched up to expose as much of his dark skin as possible while still being at least a little modest. Hiding himself wasn't needed around me since I'd seen him naked about a half dozen times now. Maybe he'd done it just in case one of the cleaning crew had come by and peeked into the open room.

"Hey," I said as I kicked off my sneakers and then pulled down my tight jeans. They were special jeans meant to be ridden in, with some extra padding because of it, but he didn't know I rode horses. He didn't know anything about me, actually. I was naked underneath, and I pulled a condom out of the back pocket before joining him on the bed.

"Did you have any trouble finding the hotel?"

PG liked to change the location of our hookups each time, but they were always in a hotel, and always a really nice one too. We could have gotten together at any cheap motel or in the back of my car, like the other guys I screwed from the app we both used. But he was classier than that.

I shook my head. "Golden isn't that far from me, so it was easy." He didn't know where I lived, so I could have been lying, and I kind of was depending on his definition of close. I'd driven over an hour from Castle Rock to get to him today, but as he was always worth it, I didn't think twice about agreeing to be with him when his request had come in.

He moved the sheet aside, exposing his thick cock and the soft patch of dark hair at its base. I was pretty free from hair without even trying, but I was also twenty-five. If I had to guess, PG was somewhere in his late forties or early fifties, judging by the trace bits of gray in his short black curls.

I slid over his lap, and he settled his hands loosely on my hips. While I smiled at him, I let his tip kiss my entrance before I moved my hand there and removed my plug. I tossed it on the floor to be retrieved later.

He didn't look surprised by me having one in. He shouldn't have been either after knowing me in this capacity for so many months. "How long were you wearing it this time?"

"Three days."

PG didn't ask me if it had been three days straight—minus bathroom breaks—probably because he knew me better than that. I generally didn't go more than a day without meeting someone from the app, and since my profile was public, anyone who was curious enough could see my activity.

He tightened his fingers on my bony hips, and I felt eagerness coursing through him. I had been looking at his profile too and knew he'd been busy, just as I had been, so it was nice to know I was still wanted.

I made quick work of spreading the prelubricated condom over his cock. Sliding onto him was easy because I'd been stretched already. That was one way I controlled these hookups. If I was always ready, there was no way anyone could go too fast with me.

I ground into him, moving my hips until I found the right angle—and pace—that worked for me. After months of seeing him, I knew it was how we did things. When he was on the bed, I rode him and got to find my climax on my own. Sometimes it felt like I was using him, slapping our bodies together and knowing I wasn't giving him exactly what he wanted, but it never took long for me to come. He liked to be in control and be a bit rougher with me.

Resting one hand on his chest, I wrapped the other around my cock, which had been painfully hard while I'd thought about him on the highway up there. I whimpered as I fought back my orgasm, trying to hang on just a little while longer. I should have jacked off before getting in my car. Then maybe I would have lasted more than a few minutes with his cock rubbing perfectly against my prostate in the most delicious way possible. But PG sent me over the edge as he moved his hands from my hips to tug on my nipples. A bit of pain was my thing. Not anything hardcore, but just enough to send that zap of energy coursing through me. It was a bit of a shock, since I was never sure how he was going to give me that extra bit of a boost, but he usually did.

PG grabbed my ass and turned me over while I was still coming down from my climax, which had ended up over his chest and stomach. He pushed my legs back toward my chest and slammed into me while I was still limp under him. Unlike a lot of guys, he didn't say someone else's name while he was fucking me. He generally didn't say anything at all. Just a bunch of grunts and groans to let me know he was enjoying me as much as I'd loved having him.

He kissed me as I lay under him. It was the only time we ever kissed. He was needy and rough, biting my lips as he panted into the kisses. Once I had control of my hands again, I brought my fingers up and ran them through his hair. His tight curls were coarse but also soft at the ends, like he had used some expensive conditioner but it had become less effective this late in the evening, nearly eight o'clock.

He met my gaze a second before he came with a loud groan, and though I would never tell him, I liked seeing the vulnerability in his dark brown eyes as he climaxed. He'd come, so he stopped kissing me. He pulled out, tossed the condom aside, and rolled away from me all within a few seconds.

We lay there together for a while, panting and trying to catch our breaths. I was the first to get up. I went to my plug and put it back in with the help of some lube I kept on me at all times, then pulled on my jeans. They were harder to get on than they had been to take off because I was so sweaty, but I managed anyway. When I put my feet in my sneakers, I found PG watching me with a smile on his face. He'd moved the pillows behind his head, propping himself up a little.

"You know you can stay and shower here, right?" he asked.

I shrugged before I pulled on my shirt. "Yeah. I know. You've told me that before. But I'm good. Not staying around isn't just a thing I do with you." I'd learned better than to be clingy in the few years I'd used the app to get my needs taken care of.

PG chuckled and sat up in bed. He really did look good naked. He'd taken care of himself well. As he stood and headed toward the bathroom, he walked with grace and none of the clumsiness I was used to seeing from guys my age. "Are we to the first name stage yet?"

I wasn't sure. Maybe we were. I figured there was no harm in him knowing just that much about me. "Eli."

"Grayson."

Which meant his full name might have been Grayson Pendleton, judging by his screenname on Hot Guy Hookups. Not that I cared. His name made him sound rich and powerful. Maybe he was some kind of secret billionaire who liked doing the hookup thing on the side. What he did or didn't do really didn't matter to me. He was sexy and I liked coming with him. That was it.

"See you," I said, waving as I backed away toward the door. This part was always a bit awkward for me. Come in, get naked, have sex—those were the parts I could handle. The afterward part where he told me I could shower and now we knew each other's names? That was weird. I liked my sex somewhere between strangers and glory holes. I hoped Grayson wasn't going to want to get to know me or anything like that. I didn't do that anymore. My lines were definitely drawn far before we would ever get to be anything close to friends.

He smiled at me again. "Take care. I'll message you the next time I'm in town."

"Sounds like a plan." I ducked out of the hotel room as I heard him turning on the shower.

Sex generally made me feel better, looser, and far more energized. If it wasn't a Wednesday night, and if I didn't have a home evaluation for the horse rescue I worked for in the morning, I would have probably gone to a club. As it was, I headed back to my apartment, which was stupid expensive. And now that my year lease was up in two weeks, I was sure the owner was going to be increasing the rent once I went month-to-month.

It wasn't a prospect I was looking forward to since I could barely afford to live there as it was. But rent was skyrocketing all over the Denver metro area, and even though I'd looked for a cheaper place, they didn't exist unless I wanted a roommate. Which I definitely didn't. They came with complications. I'd fallen hard for every guy I'd ever tried to share a place with, and that just couldn't be me anymore.

I lived on the ground-level apartment alone, unless the pictures of horses counted. Then I had fifty-two friends, all horses that I'd either helped rescue from bad situations or placed into good homes. I had a few human friends too, but not ones who generally came to my apartment. We hit the gay clubs in downtown Denver together or we hung out at the barn after work. But we didn't really all get together at my place and drink beers and watch the football game or anything like that.

I stripped off my shirt and tossed it into my overflowing laundry basket in the hall between my bedroom and the bathroom, where my washer and dryer were, before plopping down on my thrift-store sofa. It was cheap but comfortable. My water bottle from the night before was still on the floor next to the sofa, and I sipped it as I thought about Grayson. I was already getting hard again, and I groaned as I rolled over onto my stomach and tried to ignore my body's reaction to one of the hottest men I'd ever had sex with.

I had to be in Kiowa by eight, and then I was scheduled to be at the rescue for four hours after that, since I had paperwork and monthly checks to do. I didn't have any more time to spend thinking about Grayson that night. But my brain didn't seem to want to accept that.

It sucked that I didn't have more control of my body, but I was already practically humping the couch while thinking about having him in me again. Unlike most guys, he'd never disappointed me when we were together. Some guys were good, and then they had an off night, but I still gave them another chance. Two bad times in a row meant I didn't see them again. Which was probably why most of the guys I was with didn't get to repeat their times with me.

But Grayson was different. I rolled back over and undid my jeans so I could put my fist around my cock. I arched into my hand and groaned as I thought about how rough he liked to be with me when he pinned me down on a bed or pushed me up against a wall. I wanted him to fuck me as hard as he could, and he never shied away from that. We were sweaty and loud and had broken more than one hotel headboard. My best times were with him for sure.

I thought about his fingers on my hips, then when he pinched my nipples. Or the times when he'd dug his nails into the outside of my thighs as I'd ridden him. He was good about always letting me come first. And when I was done, he really got started. While I lay there loose and relaxed, he took me and I loved it all.

I jerked my hand over my cock and shot over my stomach while I imagined him on top of me and kissing me as if he needed me, like he always did right before he came. When I was done, and filthy again, I was finally able to get some sleep.

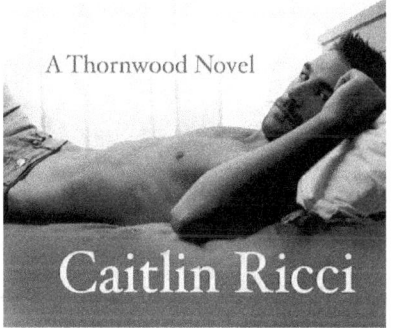

CHAPTER ONE

Caleb

I LOOKED up from unpacking the box at my feet at the sound of the doorbell ringing. It was a soft chime, which I was glad about because I hadn't thought to check it before deciding to buy the house. When the bell sounded again, I straightened up and instantly grabbed at my lower back. There was some rule about not bending over boxes and lifting with my legs instead of my bad back, but I'd apparently forgotten my doctor's orders in the move. I'd be paying for that by sundown, I was sure. I hurried to answer it, checked the peephole, and decided to open the heavy wooden door anyway, despite my better judgement. The kitchen was close, and I was pretty sure I'd managed to unpack the knives already if the cop on the other side of the door ended up being some kind of backwoods small-town Colorado murderer or something.

"Can I help you, officer?" I asked. I tried not to pay attention to how cute he was, which was damn hard given his smile. I was always a sucker for a good smile. And a cup of coffee just like the one he extended toward me.

"Hey. I'm Trent, and please don't call me 'officer' unless I'm arresting you. Everyone calls me by my first name."

I accepted the coffee and held it up so I could sniff it. I am fairly certain I sighed because he grinned at me like he was trying not to laugh. "Sorry." I was blushing pretty badly, judging by how warm the tops of my ears felt. "I haven't unpacked my coffee machine yet. Thanks for this. Is there something wrong?" I asked, because in Los Angeles cops didn't randomly come to my door unless there was trouble. I'd only been in Thornwood a day, and now I had a cop at my door. My sister, Marie, would probably love to know what kind of trouble I'd managed to get myself into so soon.

Trent shook his head, his hat slipping a little, and I was momentarily distracted by his dark hair. It was the color of chocolate, which, like my coffee, I hadn't unpacked either. I'd barely managed to get a towel out for my shower that morning after making sure my books were out on the bookshelf. "Nothing's wrong. Why? Do you think there is?"

I shrugged and sipped the coffee. Cream and sugar, which I could handle, though I normally took it black. At least he hadn't grabbed me a latte or something else that would put me in a sugar coma before lunch. "There's a cop on my front porch," I pointed out, as if my concerns needed to be explained.

"Oh!" Understanding seemed to come to him instantly. "Oh, no. I'm not here because you did something. Unless you did?"

"Not that I know of," I replied, wondering what he was doing there if it wasn't because of something I'd done.

Trent smiled at me. "Then you're fine. I just wanted to come here and introduce myself. Meet the new neighbor kind of thing."

"Really?"

"Yeah. It's a small town. So…." He shifted his weight as he leaned back on his heels. "You waiting on your family to move here too?"

I shook my head and knew why he was asking that. I'd bought a massive house, because I'd wanted to and had been able to afford it after the settlement from a car accident. But I'd probably be getting the family question fairly often until people got over their curiosity about the new guy in town. "Nope. Just me."

"Horses?"

"None of those either."

He frowned at me and turned to look over the barn and pastures that had come with the property. "You know you bought a horse farm, right?"

I laughed and took another sip of the coffee. It really was nice of him to bring it for me. "Yeah. I know. You want to come in or something?"

It was the first time I'd ever actually invited a cop into my home, not that I'd ever had anything to hide, but in LA I used to get told about probable cause and warrants all the time from my neighbors. It had been normal conversation over getting the mail. I hadn't been living in the best neighborhood at the time.

Trent chewed on his bottom lip, and damn I wanted to kiss him, but that would have been insanity. He shook his head as he stopped messing with his lip, and I got a break from thinking about kissing him for a bit. "Thanks, but I should probably be getting to work. Here's my number, in case you need something." He dug a business card out of his pocket and put his coffee down on my porch to write his number on it.

I took the card, though I wasn't too sure why I did so. It wasn't like I'd be calling him or anything. "Don't you have 911 up here?" Thornwood couldn't possibly have been so tiny that the emergency services required me calling Trent up.

"Yeah, we've got 911. Where'd you think you moved to? Antarctica or something?"

He smiled again, and I barely managed to shrug while I stood there staring at him like a dumbass. Damn but he was cute in that navy-blue uniform. I wanted to see him out of it.

"Just call. And what's your name? I don't think I caught it."

I shook my head. "I didn't say it. Caleb Robinson."

"See you later, Caleb," he told me as I stepped back, ready to close the door.

"Later."

He lifted his coffee to salute me, I did the same, and then he turned on his heel and went down the curving path through my front yard to where his police car was parked next to my very old and quite rusty SUV. Which, I realized a minute after he began pulling away, had expired tags. Damn. I tensed up, waiting for him to notice, but he didn't stop. Instead he just waved to me, I waved back at him, and then he was gone, and I went back to my morning of unpacking boxes and trying to move stuff around.

I'd never had a house this big, with five bedrooms and three bathrooms. A dozen acres spread around me, and I had no plans for any of it. Mostly I'd just wanted to get away from LA, from my life there, from everything that reminded me of that place.

I hadn't always hated it, though. I was a graphic designer, and I liked the busy lifestyle and the colors there. But dating my married boss had sort of put a damper on my love affair with the city.

My phone rang, and I hurried over to it, expecting to hear from my sister sometime that day, and instead seeing a familiar name staring back at me. "Hi." I swallowed thickly. "I didn't think I'd hear from you again."

"Hey. How's life in the mountains?" Paul asked. I'd had two months away from him, two months since I'd last been in his bed, since I'd last told him I loved him. I could still feel the scrape of his teeth on my collarbone and his fingertips digging into my hips as he fucked me.

"Thornwood isn't really in the mountains. More like the foothills," I said. I tried to keep things casual, to keep my voice light. But when I looked down at my hand on the island, I saw I was gripping it so hard my knuckles were white. I stepped back and shook out my hand. "I thought we'd agreed not to talk again."

"I know we did. But that was then and this is now. You've had some time to cool off. Give me another chance. I want to talk to you again. Why won't you let me?"

I sighed and flopped down on the couch, a foldout sofa bed monster I'd had since college, and looked out at the pine trees just beyond the huge windows that had made me fall in love with the house as soon as I walked in.

"Because...." I struggled to come up with a reasonable explanation that I hadn't already told him, but since there wasn't one, I went with the first. It hadn't worked last year when I tried to break it off with him though, so I wasn't sure why I brought it up again. "Because you were never going to leave your wife for me."

I heard Paul slam something, and this time I didn't jump, like I'd done all the time back in LA. "Caleb, you knew that. From the start of this, you knew I wasn't going to leave her. Her father owns the design firm. He pays my salary. He paid yours. My life would have been over if I'd left her."

I knew all of this, having heard it many times in the past. We'd been together for a while, nearly three years, and I thought I loved him. He'd said it often enough to me as well.

"Look, I'll be coming through Denver next month to meet with some new clients. Can I see you?"

There was so much hope in his voice, and I was tempted to give in, to tell him that he could come over, that I'd be waiting right here for him like I always was. But this was a new start for me. I'd chosen to move, to get on with my life, and I'd done it in a big way. I hadn't simply quit my job, or moved to a place he hadn't been in; I moved to another state. Another time zone even.

"I don't think so. Not this time," I said. And I was proud of myself for saying no, just this once. That had taken a lot for me to be able to do.

"Why not?"

I closed my eyes, then pinched the bridge of my nose. But my glasses got in the way and I ended up stabbing the little plastic pads into the corners of my eyes instead. Glasses were a new experience for me since more often than not I wore my contacts, but I hadn't felt like putting them in this morning when my eyes were so dry from the Colorado air. I desperately needed to pick up a humidifier to fix that.

"Because it's not a good idea. Because I'm not going to be the other man again. Not anymore. The sex was good, but I can't do it anymore. I want a real relationship and not one that involves being called into lunch meetings so you can get your dick sucked as I hide under the desk in case anyone happens to walk by."

He laughed as if he thought I was joking. Too bad I wasn't. At first it had been a little sexy, maybe, to have this kind of secret thing going on. I wasn't some innocent, naive person, though. I'd known who he was, and who his wife was, the first time we kissed while working late on a project. But somehow I'd been dumb enough to believe that he'd eventually realize I was better for him than she was. I hadn't taken into account how much more he loved his money than he cared about either her or me apparently.

"I'm being serious," I told him when he was still laughing at my nonexistent joke.

That shut him up quickly. "Oh. Well, why don't I come visit you, and we can see how we work out like that? You could be my Colorado love affair."

Saying no to that was easy, but the way he offered it made me wonder something. I should have asked it a long time ago, but I hadn't, and I wasn't sure why. Maybe I'd been too scared, too worried about the answer to find out for sure. But that wasn't the case any longer. "How many other men were you having sex with while we were together?" I asked in a clipped tone, because I was sure I wasn't the only one. Not with how he so easily suggested that I be his Colorado affair, like he had a guy waiting for him in every state. He likely did actually.

"Caleb…. C'mon, you know it's not like that. You were special to me. You still are."

"How many others?" I asked. "More than ten? More than twenty?"

He took a long time answering me. "Thirty-six, I guess. I haven't really kept track."

"Jesus fucking Christ!" I suddenly felt really ill, and I was glad I'd been getting tested regularly for all of my adult life.

"Caleb, that's just a number. You know they didn't mean anything to me. They—"

I shook my head. "Paul, stop. It's over. It was over between us when I quit my job, it was over when your wife hit me with her car after finding out about us, it was over when I left California, and it sure as hell is over now! Don't try to call me again. I won't pick up. Just… damn. Go get some help or something. Bye."

I hung up my phone before he could say anything else to me, and I was glad I had, because soon enough I was bent over my toilet heaving up the coffee Trent had brought me, which was the only thing I'd bothered to have so far that morning. Lucky for me.

After my throw-up session, I desperately needed a hot shower too. I couldn't believe it. Well, actually I probably could. Paul was smooth and slick like a model in a magazine. I'd been falling all over myself around him since the first time he touched my hand when I went in for an interview.

Saying yes to him the first time wasn't hard to do. And it got easier as we went along. Sex in his office, in his car, in a hotel, in my apartment… they were all normal parts of my life with him. He would send me a text saying he needed a file brought over, and a location, and I would be there.

I'd missed parties with friends, phone calls from my sister, and important meetings with my own clients just to be his fuck toy basically. It hurt to realize that now, but for once I was finally thinking with a clear head, and things were actually looking up for me, now that I didn't have Paul Diggs around to screw with my thoughts and my body.

It was a good feeling to be free of him, and when I'd gotten cleaned up, I was ready to go explore Thornwood. I'd brought food with me, of a sort, in the form of beef jerky, bottles of soda, and granola bars. But now I was hungry for something real. I felt a little bad for leaving a pile of boxes half-unpacked in the middle of what would be a gorgeous living room once my clutter and broken pieces of cardboard were removed. But then again, this was my house now, my first house, the first time I hadn't been living in an apartment, and if I wanted to leave cardboard boxes lying around, then I could. I was able to leave them there for weeks if I chose to. Uh, actually, no I couldn't. That would drive me nuts. But I could wait to unpack the rest of them for a little while. I'd been pushing hard to get through them all in one day. I could take a little break. And my back was really sore too. I rubbed at it as I walked down the narrow, winding path that went from my front door to the driveway. Another path went to an old garage, but I didn't think I'd be using it all that often until it got really cold and snowy. My SUV was good off-road—it had perpetual mud on it—and I couldn't remember a time when I'd ever kept it in a garage except for at work. And I hadn't made enough to make that an affordable everyday option.

My SUV and I bumped along the uneven dirt driveway that ran into my property until it met up with a paved two-lane road, which I understood to be the main street going through Thornwood. Tiny towns were new to me, but I absolutely loved the lack of traffic as I signaled out of habit, then pulled onto the road. I turned on some classic rock—my favorite—and kept to the speed limit as much as I could since the way was a bit twisty and I didn't really know my way all that well.

I passed by what looked like a pretty nice horse property a few miles down the road with a sign saying they gave lessons and offered boarding. There was even a sign for an upcoming competition, which made me think of my nephews, who were all big into showing their horses. It wasn't something I'd ever been interested in, and my sister hadn't been either, but I guessed her husband was in a big way. I wasn't all that close to him, probably because the only thing we had in common was my sister and the kids, but I'd been trying. Now that I had a house, I planned to invite them out to spend some time there. I was pretty sure I'd get tired of having three boys running around my home pretty quickly. I wasn't really big on kids for the most part, but since I hadn't seen them since before the oldest one started kindergarten, and now he was a teenager, I thought I probably should. They were my nephews after all, and I missed my sister.

I drove into what I figured was the town proper, which was little more than ten stores all together on either side of the street, parking spots in front of them, and signs for more parking behind the stores in the aspens. I saw a mechanic, a bank, a drug store, a craft place, a pet store, which promised the lowest prices of tropical fish around, a fishing store with live bait, and then, at the end of the row and with the most cars circled around it, a fifties era-looking diner complete with aluminum accents and neon lights.

I parked in front of the diner, which was called Rosie's, and headed inside. Seating was tight, but I got a space at a high bar with people sitting on stools on either side of me. Like a typical diner, the place was loud, but the food looked great—or maybe that was because I was starving. Either way I needed a bacon cheeseburger right away.

After my food came and some of my need dissipated as I took big bites of my burger and shoved fries into my mouth, I looked around the diner and noticed a familiar face. The only person I knew in town was talking with some other cops in a booth. When he saw me looking, I waved to him, he waved back, and I returned to my burger. The food was great, with just the right amount of grease coming out of my thick burger patty and dripping down my fingers as I ate. I knew I'd be back there regularly, and not just because it looked to be the only place in town to eat out. From where I was seated, with big windows a few seats down from me, I could see a small grocery store tucked behind some of the aspens farther on through town, which was great because that meant I could get frozen pizzas to keep on hand. I wouldn't be doing much cooking. I just wasn't all that good at it. Thankfully I already had design jobs line up from clients back in LA who were just waiting for me to open my books and become available again. I'd be booked solid again in a month, I was sure of it, and that was a good feeling.

I'd always loved to create beautiful things for other people, but doing so while also worrying about my relationship with Paul had been a bit of a mess. Now I could do my job and make banners and websites for people without having to worry about any complications like that.

"Hey, Caleb."

I looked up to see Trent standing next to me. "Hi." I wiped my mouth with my napkin and wanted to invite him to sit down, but the seats around me were full of people eating lunch just like I was. "On break?" I asked instead.

He nodded. "Yeah. Glad you made it out of your house to come mingle with the townsfolk."

I smiled and he smiled back at me. "It's good food."

"Better be. Rosie was my mom."

I thought he was joking at first, but he just kept looking at me, and I slowly realized he wasn't joking at all. "Wow. Uh, congrats."

"Thanks."

"Trent, we gotta go! Break's over, kid!" one of the guys with him called.

Trent turned and waved to them but not before I could see him blushing, maybe at being called a kid. He couldn't have been that far from my own age of thirty-two, but maybe since the guys with him looked to be in their fifties, that was why they referred to him with that particular appellation.

"See you around," I told him.

He nodded. "Yeah. You will."

There was nothing ominous in the way he'd said it, just a simple, yes, I would. Probably because he was a cop and they were pretty active in the small town. He touched my shoulder as he left, nothing too major but enough for me to know he'd done it. I brushed it off, figuring it was a small town and people were probably pretty friendly.

But after I was done with lunch and spent some time walking around the town, I was thinking about it and wondering why he'd touched me like that. It was hard for me not to wonder, but as I drove back to my new house to tackle the boxes in my living room a few hours later, it started to get easier to forget about the touch and move on.

I found a picture of my sister and her kids and put it up on my bookcase in the living room, right next to my copy of the biography of Harvey Milk. I had romances galore, a lot of them historicals, under that shelf, but that was where I kept my important stuff. I put a geode next to the book, a small one, barely more than two inches wide, that I'd held on to since the first boy I ever kissed had given it to me. Right before his dad had broken us apart, then moved him to the other side of the country. I'd been thirteen.

A little jade elephant—a gift from my sister that she'd found in a shop in Thailand well before she met Dan and had the kids—was placed next to her picture. She'd traveled the world while I was getting my degree in design. I'd been jealous of her, but she was just as jealous of me when she went back to school after her travels, only to find out that she was the oldest person in her freshman class. And though some of the teachers liked her, none of the guys in her classes did.

With my bookshelf done, I had one more box I could recycle in the morning. It was a long drive to the nearest dump that had a recycling center, close to half an hour, but I didn't want to throw them away, and I couldn't stand all the clutter. I'd had movers to help me with the big stuff, but I'd gone from an apartment to a huge house and most of my big stuff fit in one room. I'd been sleeping on the fold-out couch in the living room since my futon stopped flipping back up to a couch a few months back, and as I sat down on it and groaned, I realized I really didn't want to do any more moving, ever. I hated it. Not only was I not fit enough to carry heavy boxes everywhere, but my back hurt from bending over for even a short amount of time. If I wasn't careful with it, my doctor in LA had told me, I'd throw it out for sure. I needed to find a good chiropractor, and soon, before I wound up on the floor on my stomach, unable to move again like I had in LA.

I was mostly done unpacking my kitchen when I heard something get knocked over by the garage, which I brushed off without thinking much about it. I really only heard it because I didn't have on any music. Otherwise the house was completely silent except for me moving things around. I needed to get my TV hooked up right away to fix that. I couldn't stand the quiet after living for so long in the city.

But I heard the noise again, and after freezing and wondering where it came from, I walked over to the big windows across from my sofa bed to check if I could see anything outside. I couldn't exactly see the garage, and even if I could, it was dark out and I didn't have any outside lights.

I had been used to sleeping by the light of an overhead streetlamp across from me that lit up the parking lot where impounded vehicles were taken. I shook my head as I realized, for the first time really, that moving here had not been my smartest idea ever. I didn't even own a flashlight.

I heard something coming from the garage again and dug my phone out of my pocket to call 911. I probably should have too, but

I pulled out Trent's card with his number on it, and suddenly I was dialing him while I crouched beside my window and hoped that whoever it was out there hadn't seen me standing in my living room all alone with the lights on behind me.

"Hello, this is Trent," he answered on the third ring.

"Trent!" I hissed into the phone as I covered it and my mouth with my hand to muffle the sound of my voice. "It's Caleb—"

"I know who you are. There aren't that many people in this town that I can't remember the voices of. What's wrong?"

I heard him getting up, and the sound of a bed squeaking, and I winced, hoping I hadn't woken him up or interrupted something. It was only nine, but maybe he had to be up early. I wanted to hang up, to tell him I'd only been imagining something being by my garage, but then I thought back to every single horror movie that took place in a cabin in the woods where not one of those stupid kids ever called a cop at the first sign of something going wrong. Well, I had a cop on the phone with me right then, and I wasn't going to end up hacked into a bunch of little pieces if I could help it. "There's someone outside my house—"

"I'll be right there. Where are you? Are you safe?"

I couldn't tell if having him sounding genuinely worried about me was a good thing or not. "I'm in my living room, kneeling on the floor and trying not to be seen."

"Good. I'm getting in my car now. I'll check it out, then come up to the house. Stay on the phone with me."

"Okay, okay. I can do that." Breathing became easier as I relaxed a little bit. Trent was coming, he had a gun, and he would take care of whatever it was. "But what if it's a bear?" He couldn't possibly hold off a bear with just a gun.

He laughed, and I heard the sound of his car as he started driving. "If it's a bear, we've both got big problems."

"Well that's not reassuring at all," I grumbled.

"Wasn't supposed to be. I'm coming down the hill now. I'll be there in just a few minutes."

I nodded and licked my lips as I pressed my hand against the cold glass window. "Be careful."

CAITLIN RICCI was fortunate growing up to be surrounded by family and teachers who encouraged her love of reading. She has always been a voracious reader and that love of the written word easily morphed into a passion for writing. If she isn't writing, she can usually be found studying as she works toward her counseling degree. She comes from a military family, and the men and women of the armed forces are close to her heart. She also enjoys gardening, hiking, and horseback riding in the Colorado Rockies she calls home with her wonderful fiancé and their two dogs. Her belief that there is no one true path to happily ever after runs deeply through all of her stories.

Website: www.CaitlinRicci.com

Prince Jai, a merciless vampire warlord, has taken up a crusade to stop the enslavement of the humans and werewolves by his own kind. He's heard tales of the time before a comet came and changed the world, and though they may just be stories told by an old human woman, he finds hope in them. After months of killing the other vampires, he's nearing his goal of taking the king's throne for himself. It's the only way to bring peace to everyone, and he won't stop until he sees that happen.

However, his men are tired, and when one clan proves to be too much for him, he agrees to a temporary peace treaty. To sweeten the deal, Jai is given the use of a blood slave, Ash. Jai detests the use of blood slaves and wants nothing to do with them. But when he realizes Ash could be another weapon in his arsenal, he spends the months training him to be everything his master has ever feared.

www.dreamspinnerpress.com

College student Milo Brickman is in a bind as he tries to figure out how he's supposed to afford a master's degree. His best friend points him to an ad looking for guys to star in light kink scenes. It's good money and his friend has worked for the company before, so Milo gives it a shot. On the job, Milo meets porn veteran Sullivan Craine, who Milo falls for—hard.

When Milo and Sullivan are thrown together for a scene all about denying Milo pleasure, Milo is desperate for more by the time the director yells, "Wrap!" Convincing Sullivan he's okay with a boyfriend who is not only much older than him, but who's made a career in porn, is a tough sell—but one that Milo is determined to make.

www.dreamspinnerpress.com

A Planet Called Wish: Book One

The Intergalactic Star Pilot Academy has accepted Thierry Leroux into the elite class of sky year 2231. But the academy comes with a hefty price tag, and there's no way he, a poor Sythe orphan, has the credits the academy requires. Thierry's brother, Corbin, a high-class companion, suggests Thierry sell his virginity for the cost of tuition. It seems like a ridiculous idea, but it may be Thierry's only shot, so Thierry asks Corbin to arrange a meeting on the pleasure planet of Wish.

On Wish, Thierry meets Corbin's boss, Monroe, and they agree to auction off Thierry's virginity. Thierry is grateful to the masked buyer he knows only as "Dragonfly," and Dragonfly is gentle, making Thierry's first time a good memory. When Dragonfly requests to see him again, and pay for the pleasure, Thierry returns to Wish. But in this game, falling in love is dangerous for the heart, and Thierry might not like the man behind the mask.

www.dreamspinnerpress.com

A Planet Called Wish: Book Two

For two decades Corbin Leroux has worked on the planet Wish as a high-priced companion. He loves his life where physical pleasure is encouraged and has no intention of quitting it. Corbin sees his clients almost as part of his family. Not even when bounty hunter Emmanuel Leoniste comes to kill him will Corbin roll over and give up his lifestyle.

Despite being a hired killer, Emmanuel lives by a strict moral code. Killing whores is acceptable, and easy. Or it was until he met up with Corbin. Worn down by the pesky Corbin's resolve, Emmanuel accepts Corbin's bribe and calls off the hit. But the truce might not last. Emmanuel's mounting desire for Corbin causes problems. He refuses to allow anyone close enough to become intimate with him, especially someone like Corbin. Yet with each smile and soft kiss, Emmanuel's emotional shield is dismantled piece by piece.

www.dreamspinnerpress.com

www.ingramcontent.com/pod-product-compliance
Lightning Source LLC
Chambersburg PA
CBHW071007280626
47160CB00015B/1691